Christmas Love Quiz
(taken by Anne Hyden)

1) **The perfect kiss should make you:**
a) Feel as if you'd nipped too much eggnog
b) Faint in his strong arms
c) Wonder if you fed your goldfish this morning

2) **Mr. Right is:**
a) Everything you've ever dreamed of
b) Everything Mom warned you against
c) Anyone you won't fall in love with

3) **If you could marry any man in the world, it would be:**
a) A nice, dull man who'll have you despite your secret
b) A handsome, sexy rancher who kisses devastatingly
c) b) is the only answer!

Dear Reader,

If Santa told you that the man of your dreams would be waiting under the tree this year, *who* would you unwrap on Christmas morning? A secret crush? Your husband? Tommy Lee Jones? If you'll send me a postcard with a brief (20 words max.) description of your answer, signed with your first name and your city and state, you just might see it printed with others on a special page in the months to come.

This holiday season, though, Santa's busy searching for the man of Sharon's dreams in Hayley Gardner's novel, *Holiday Husband.* The single Scrooge has challenged St. Nick to deliver Mr. Right by December 25. And on Christmas Eve something tall, dark and handsome is coming down the chimney.

But Anne, in Laurie Paige's *Christmas Kisses for a Dollar,* has to avoid meeting the man of her dreams—or else. She'll only date the dullest men her tiny Texas town has to offer. The worse a man kisses, the better! And rancher Jon Sinclair, who doesn't like *or elses,* kisses a little too well....

I hope you enjoy these two holiday treats. Next month, look for two Yours Truly titles by Janice Kaiser and Christie Ridgway—two new novels about unexpectedly meeting, dating...and marrying Mr. Right.

Happy Holidays!

Melissa Senate
Editor

Please address questions and book requests to:
Silhouette Reader Service
U.S.: 3010 Walden Ave., P.O. Box 1325, Buffalo, NY 14269
Canadian: P.O. Box 609, Fort Erie, Ont. L2A 5X3

LAURIE PAIGE

Christmas Kisses for a Dollar

Published by Silhouette Books
America's Publisher of Contemporary Romance

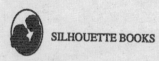

SILHOUETTE BOOKS

ISBN 0-373-52009-3

CHRISTMAS KISSES FOR A DOLLAR

Copyright © 1995 by Olivia M. Hall

Printed in U.S.A.

About the author

At our family reunion last year, my sister reminded me that I used to make up stories and insist that she write them down so I could share them with the whole family. The stories were two pages long and involved great adventures that ended when the heroine returned home. "And they were so happy to see her that her mom didn't scold her for being late to dinner," was the way the stories usually ended. She also pointed out that I'm no longer four years old, but I'm still making up stories!

What can I say? I love romance. I rejoice in happy endings. I'm jubilant when they finally say "I do."

Marriage isn't only a grand adventure, but the foundation of civilization. Men would still be living in caves and running around in bearskin rugs if it weren't for women. We bravely confront, tame and soothe the savage beasts...not to mention putting up with whole evenings devoted to channel surfing and toothpaste tubes squeezed in the middle!

Laurie Paige has written over twenty-five books for Silhouette. Watch for her next story coming from Silhouette Special Edition during spring 1996!

This book is for Tara, who said, "Yes, you can"
after I explained all the reasons I couldn't.
With thanks and warm fuzzies.

1

Christmas Kisses—$1.00

Jonathan Sinclair smiled at the provocative banner wafting in the December breeze. The sign, attached to two trees, floated over a booth wreathed in holly and cedar boughs. The occasion appeared to be an old-fashioned bazaar in the school yard.

He stopped at a red light and used the opportunity to assess the group waiting to buy a kiss. The line was long. He couldn't see the woman from this angle, but the guys were young—some of them teenagers, he guessed, in line on a dare from their friends, most likely—while the rest were probably in their twenties, maybe thirties.

All single, he assumed. They didn't have the look of men who were shackled to shrews, which, from his observations of life, were what women became once they got a man to the altar.

Or even before, as his own experience proved.

A shudder ran clear down to his toes as he remembered his close call in this very town. He'd been eighteen when the girl next door, who'd been twenty, had tried to trap him into marriage with the oldest trick in the book. Few people had believed he'd been innocent as he'd claimed.

It had been a learning experience. He went on the alert when women came on to him in too friendly a manner, and he suspected ulterior motives behind their smiles.

The light changed. He waited with resigned patience for the crowd to amble past the lined crosswalk. When the street was clear, he turned the corner.

Everyone in the county was in town for the festivities, it seemed. He grimaced at his poor timing and looked for a parking space near the feed-and-seed store. The fertilizer he'd ordered last week was in. All he wanted was to pick it up and get back to the ranch.

The ranch. Three hundred acres of pines and pasture, two hundred head of cattle and a commercial plant nursery.

He'd never expected to inherit the place although he'd loved it as a kid. He'd lit out on his own right after high school, off to see the world. His parents had been upset, but they hadn't tried to stop him. They'd understood his restlessness.

Sorrow momentarily overshadowed the bright day. They'd died last spring in a flash flood, a known hazard in Texas. He still couldn't believe they were gone. Life was short....

He directed his thoughts to the present. He intended to revive the successful ranch operation his grandfather had run. Once the place was booming again, he'd sell the whole works, make some money and head out for parts unknown.

That was what he was good at—fixing up a run-down enterprise and selling it at a profit, then moving on. He'd learned to do that well in the years he'd been on his own and had made a good-size fortune by speculating in floundering companies. Of course he'd lost a bundle, too.

He spotted a parking space and whipped into it before the guy in the fancy car who was also eyeing the spot could beat him to it. With a triumphant grin of one-upmanship, Jon leapt to the ground from the pickup.

The breeze, straight off the Gulf of Mexico, gave him a damp caress. He'd been living in the far west where spit dried before it hit the ground. Here, thirty miles up Highway 12 from Beaumont, Texas, the air was humid year-round. It took a while to get used to that again.

Laughter from the cowboys lined up for the kisses caught his attention. He paused and glanced over the bed of the pickup to see what was going on...and stopped dead still. Then he simply stared at the woman who stood in the booth.

She was the loveliest, sexiest creature he'd ever seen.

Her hair was black—pure raven black. The sun glinted off it with no hints of red or blond in the deep waves that cascaded over her shoulders. It invited a man to sink his hands into it, to tangle his fingers in the long, shiny strands...to use it to hold her while he dropped kisses all over her mouth.

Her smile was radiant, her lips full and luscious. She wore a rosy-red lipstick, but he was willing to bet the color in her cheeks was natural.

It was her eyes that made her irresistible. They were blue with a touch of gray and maybe violet. He couldn't tell for sure from this distance. Her lashes were long and black, weighting the lids and giving her a languorous air...as if she'd recently climbed out of bed after making the most tempestuous love a man could imagine.

His body surged to life at the thought.

Yeah, he could see what the big attraction was. If the line hadn't been so long, he might have been tempted to join it.

Shaking his head at his own foolishness, he crossed the street to the store. It was locked. The sign in the window said the owner was at the bazaar and would open again at one.

Jon glanced at his watch. Five after twelve. He might as well eat lunch. If anything was open. For all he knew, the whole town had closed down to attend the event.

He headed across the street toward the school yard where there were several food booths. He spotted a hot-dog stand run by the rotary club. A sign explained that the proceeds of the bazaar were to go to a new gym for the local school. Well, he'd do his part for the community effort.

Another sweep of laughter sounded from the kissing booth. He paused in the shade of an oak tree about twenty feet away and watched as a bashful youth was egged on by his friends to take his kiss. When the boy handed over the dollar, the Venus in the kissing booth caught the kid by the ears and gave him a loud buss on the cheek. The boy blushed as red as the boiled shrimp on display at the seafood booth, but tossed his friends a proud grin as he strutted toward them across the lawn.

Heat swept over Jon and set a flame in his nether parts. There were certain circumstances during which he didn't mind a woman holding on to his ears, either. He unobtrusively ran a hand down the front of his jeans to make sure he wasn't about to bust his zipper. Good thing he'd put on briefs that morning.

He glanced at the hot-dog booth, pulled out his wallet, checked his money—he had six twenties—and gave a mental shrug. It was only money and it was for a good cause. He headed for the kissing line, tucking a bill into his shirt pocket as he went.

The guy in front of him was grinning like a weasel who'd found a hole in the henhouse as he waited for his turn to kiss the black-haired Venus. Jon disliked the man on sight.

"Hoo-wee," the jerk said. "I'm gonna enjoy this."

"Do you know who she is?" Jon asked.

"Yeah. Anne Hyden. I went to school with her. Never got a chance to get close enough to kiss her, though." The chump was obviously relishing the thought.

A stab of irritation hit Jon. He suppressed it. "She have a steady or something back then?"

"Nah." The guy frowned as he searched through his memory. "She didn't date nobody. Too good for the locals, I guess. Her uncle was the mayor. He still is. I figured she'd marry some rich guy when she went off to a fancy school up north, but she didn't. I hear she's been seeing a senator."

Jon rolled the name over his tongue. Anne... Anne Hyden. He liked it. He observed her as she accepted the quick, dry kisses with an easy humor and a no-nonsense manner.

The blood stirred aggressively in his groin area as he thought of how he'd like to kiss her... wet and deep and sensual, with lips and tongue and hands all involved. None of this namby-pamby, closed-mouth stuff.

Not that he would do that here in front of a crowd. After all, he had some finesse.

But it was something to think about while he waited his turn. He grinned. It wouldn't be long. She kept the line moving at a rapid clip with her friendly little smooches and teasing remarks to the men, all of whom she seemed to know.

Of course, to live in a town the size of Richport for a week, and not know everyone, would be difficult.

"I don't see how the mayor can put up with that kind of display," a feminine voice remarked.

Jon peered under the oak branch and spied two young matrons sitting in the shade on the other side of the tree. He grinned at the look of sour grapes on the face of the plump woman who was fanning herself furiously while she and her friend gossiped.

"Well, she did bring in the most money in the shortest time last year," the other woman replied. "And the pastor of the Methodist church was the first in line this morning."

"Humph," remarked the first woman, her fan swishing back and forth in rampant disapproval.

The line moved forward. Jon settled his white Stetson firmly on his head as the breeze kicked up a few dust swirls along the side of the road. Two more in front of him.

Then it was the jerk's turn. Jon found himself tensing for action the way he used to when he worked as a bouncer in a bar, which had been his first job after leaving home. With an effort, he relaxed his shoulders and his stance.

The guy in front of him handed over his dollar. He reached both hands out and grabbed the smiling Venus by the waist. A flicker of emotion darted through her eyes. Jon tensed again.

"Well, Snooze Allyn," she said brightly, laying a hand against the guy's chest. "Are you still napping after lunch the way you used to in Mrs. Brown's English class?"

Jon relaxed when the jerk's ears turned red. The lout let go of her waist. "Nah. My boss don't like it."

She wrinkled her nose. "Yeah, bosses are like that." She held up her cheek to him. He dipped and took a quick peck at it, then ambled off with a cocky grin.

Jon saw the suppressed amusement in her eyes before she turned to him. "Violet," he said.

"I beg your pardon?" Her expression became inquiring and, he thought, wary. Several emotions flickered through the intriguing depths. She pressed a hand against her chest as if disturbed by something.

His voice dropped to a husky murmur. "Your eyes. Blue with gray and a touch of violet. It's a lethal combination."

He couldn't believe he'd said that...and in the sexiest voice he'd ever used on a woman—low and vibrant, as if they were already making love. A wave of hunger swept over him, stronger than anything he'd ever felt.

Her smile wavered for an instant, then reasserted itself. "You're holding up the line," she informed him. "Let's see the color of your money, cowboy, else you'll have to step aside."

He placed the folded bill in her outstretched hand and pushed his hat out of the way. "Let me know when I've used this up," he said and reached for her.

Anne glanced at the twenty he laid in her hand. Her heart started pounding again, the way it had when she'd first spied him staring at her from the shade of the old oak tree. His gaze had been so intent, fathoms deep and similar to the look of a hunter on the prowl. It had intrigued her and sent sensations spiraling into the innermost parts of her.

She scowled as her imagination went haywire, offering up all sorts of exotic wonders as she looked at his mouth. If he was determined to get his money's worth, the kiss would go on rather long, the inane thought came to her.

Dumbfounded, she watched while he bent his head toward her. She got a glimpse of dark hair slanting across the brow of a narrow face with a strong chin, a thin nose and eyes that were silvery gray with a blue-gray line around the iris.

Staring into his eyes, she found she couldn't look away. His gaze was intense…passionate…and other things she couldn't name. Who was he?

She found herself caught up in a pair of arms that felt as strong and ropy as rawhide. The cowboy was on the slender side, an inch or so under six feet, but she sensed the strength he kept in check as his embrace pulled her forward and off-balance.

The wooden edge of the booth caught her at midthigh; then she felt heat all the way along the front of her body as she fell against the cowboy, dependent upon his strength to hold her up. She heard him give a grunt, then his arms tightened.

His lips hovered over hers, two inches away…one inch…a breath…

Alarm invaded every part of her, and for the life of her she couldn't think of anything to say that would distract him from his obvious intent to kiss her soundly.

Twenty dollars' worth!

"Don't," she finally managed in a stern tone, her heart working double time. The word hardly had time to form before his mouth touched hers. Her tongue accidentally stroked his lips.

She sensed his surprise, or maybe it was shock, for his chest surged upward against hers as he caught his breath, and his arms tightened in a convulsive embrace.

For the first time in his life, Jon forgot the basic tenet of self-preservation: Always keep your wits. Always.

When he grazed her lips and felt her tongue glide over his mouth, it was as if he'd been hit by a bolt of lightning. It burned out every thought of survival he'd ever had.

He only knew one thing: this was the woman he had to have. It was that simple.

And at the moment, that was enough—that he was holding her, kissing her. And it was the best thing he'd ever known.

She was warm and curvy in his arms, and she smelled like a summer garden after a light rain. Her fragrance wafted about them, becoming stronger as the heat between them intensified. He was drenched in hot desire.

Her hands clutched his shirt. She caught her breath and held it. Triumph flared briefly as he sensed her surprise, then the response she couldn't hide.

"Mmm," she crooned.

She slipped her hands into his hair, pulling it sharply as the passion increased. He cradled her head in one hand and took the kiss deeper, harder.

Vaguely, he heard noises around him, but the words didn't penetrate the hazy fog of delight.

Then the Venus with the midnight hair collapsed in his arms.

Startled, he took her full weight as her head tilted back and she went totally limp. He stared at her, then realization dawned. *She'd fainted.*

"Young fool," someone snarled behind him. "What do you think you're doing—manhandling her like that?"

Someone grabbed his shoulder. Jon shrugged off the hand. Bending slightly, he hoisted Anne Hyden in his arms, lifted her clear of the booth and turned.

He faced an angry mob, all glaring at him. He glared back.

"Where should I take her?" he asked a woman who pushed her way forward and bent over Anne. "Someplace quiet," he added, with a narrow-eyed warning holding off the school chum who'd kissed Anne before him.

"Her house," the woman said, releasing Anne's wrist after counting her pulse. Her eyes sparkled at him as if she found the whole incident amusing. She pointed. "Over there."

He saw a white frame house nestled among hibiscus bushes across the side street from the school. He headed for it, the older woman brushing the crowd aside to let him through. Finally, he was in the clear.

Behind him, the older woman—a nurse by her actions—ordered the line to form again and took Anne's place in the kissing booth. He heard several groans of disappointment.

An arm crept around his neck. He glanced down at the woman he held. Her eyes were still closed. Her cheeks were flushed an attractive pink, her breath came quickly between parted lips and her heart pounded. Her head slumped forward, nestling against his shoulder as if she'd often snuggled in his arms.

In his dreams, he thought, and wished they were on their way to a romantic tryst at that moment. She felt like an angel, light and ethereal, yet warm and womanly, too.

The door was open when he reached the house with its neat shrubs and flower borders. He went inside and laid the luscious burden on a comfortable-looking sofa.

He removed her shoes and swung her legs up. After putting a cushion under her head, he knelt and observed her closely, an odd anxiety constricting his chest. Surely he hadn't hurt her....

Bending, he gave her a closer perusal. "Okay," he said after a silent minute, "you can open your eyes now."

The thick black lashes fluttered, then popped up, and he stared into eyes the color of wood violets.

Anne was reluctant to give up the lovely experience of being in his arms. She placed a hand against her chest where her heart still beat in an irregular pattern. When she'd felt his lips on hers, it had nearly pounded out of her chest. Strange, to react so strongly to a kiss.

She'd reacted to him before that, she admitted. There had been a stabbing pang in her chest when she'd noticed him that first time, when he'd stood under the oak tree and watched her before making up his mind about buying a kiss.

She pulled herself together and glanced around. "Good, we're alone." She managed a wry smile.

He frowned at her. "What the hell was the fainting act about?" he demanded.

"I didn't want you to get beat up or arrested for mauling me," she explained, her sense of humor coming to the fore as her heart slowed and its beat evened out. She didn't want him to know his kiss had affected her to the point of fainting. It sounded so utterly Victorian.

She sat up and swung her legs to the side, knees bent. She saw his gaze roam their length as she tucked her skirt around them, and she felt another flutter within her chest.

"Who was going to do the honors?" he asked in a dry voice. "The jerk you went to school with?"

"Snooze?" She laughed, regaining her equilibrium at this safe topic. "No, not him."

He smiled, too, not cynically, but seemingly relaxed now that he knew she was all right. "Why would I get arrested?" he asked. "You were the one selling kisses. I was merely trying to get my money's worth."

"Twenty dollars," she murmured, curious about him. "Do you always throw money away like that?"

She licked her lips when he continued to stare at her mouth as if he were thinking of starting the kiss all over again. "I didn't consider it a waste."

"It was too intimate for a public kiss." She frowned at him. "And you didn't quit when I pulled your hair."

"I thought that was because you were excited, too." He shook his head. "That never happened to me before."

"What?"

"Getting lost in a kiss like that."

Jon took in the delicate picture she presented. The heat, which hadn't gone completely, surged anew. He wanted to strip her of the angelic outfit and find the devilish imp he detected deep in her gorgeous eyes.

"Black Irish," he murmured, mesmerized all over again.

Her eyebrows lifted in question. They were as black as her hair and lashes, with a pronounced arch like a gull's wing.

"That's what my grandmother called my grandfather. He had Irish blue eyes, but hair as black as sin. She said it was the Spanish blood that got mixed in from sailors washing ashore after the defeat of the Armada."

Anne smiled with delight at his story. She saw his silvery gaze flick to her lips once more. She remembered the taste of him when she'd tried to protest the kiss she could see coming but couldn't get the word out in time.

With an effort, she resisted an urge to lick her lips again to see if she could still taste him there. That kiss had rocked her . . . right to her toes. A first for her, too.

His mouth was intriguing. The bottom lip was slightly fuller than the top. Both were well-defined, as if outlined by the artist who'd carved him from living marble.

"Keep looking at me like that and you might go into a real faint at my next kiss."

Her heart did a tap dance against her chest. The pull was there between them. She backed off, using humor as a defense. "Yeah?" she challenged. "I'm waiting with a worm on my tongue."

His eyebrows shot up in surprise. "A what?"

"Bated breath. Haven't you been watching the reruns of 'Mork and Mindy'?"

"No. I don't have time for things like that."

"Aha. An all-work, no-play, nose-to-the-grindstone kind of guy," she mocked.

He ignored her light humor and gave her another perusal. "You have very tempting dimples."

She lifted a hand to her mouth. "I've heard them described as cute, but tempting?"

Jon sat on the sofa beside her, crowding her so that his thigh pressed against her knees. "Yes, tempting." He touched the tiny dimples that winked in and out at him as she talked or smiled. They were at the corners of her mouth. "They focus attention on your mouth. Make me think of other things I'd like to do to it . . . to you . . . with you."

The dimples winked, disappeared. "I'd advise you to curb your, uh, impulses. This town is pretty straitlaced."

He leaned closer and noticed that she didn't flinch. Brave. He liked that in a woman. "Are you?"

"I'm afraid so."

"You kissed me back."

Anne shook her head. "I did no such thing. That was an accident when I touched your lips. I was trying to tell you not to act on what I could see in your eyes."

"Which was?"

"Lust, clear as the nose on your face."

"I wasn't the only one who felt it," he insisted. "You moved your lips under mine. And your heart was beating like sixty against my chest."

For a moment, she thought of all the possibilities—falling in love, kissing, teasing, laughing, sleeping together, waking in each other's arms. Having a home, children…well, it was a lovely thought, but those things were never to be, not for her.

She had the family curse.

For a moment, the old resentment rose. Because of her heart, she hadn't been in the school band. She hadn't been a cheerleader. She hadn't played basketball or soccer.

Fragile, delicate little Anne, who mustn't become over-excited, overheated, overjoyed. Poor Anne, who'd fainted when the captain of the football team had given her a smothering kiss one time. She'd been fifteen. It had been her last date while in high school. All the guys had been afraid she'd have heart failure and her aunt would kill them because of it.

Her mother's heart had given out during childbirth. Two cousins had died from weak hearts almost at birth. She had a heart murmur, which wasn't terribly serious in itself, but it was an indication of the family trait.

She wouldn't pass it on to her children. To force them into a restricted life when all the world was there to be dis-covered, to watch them die before they'd hardly lived, to see them fall in love, marry, then die before their children had a chance to know them the way her own mother had? No, she simply wouldn't, couldn't do it.

But sometimes she thought of the possibilities….

She stifled the regret. She'd learned long ago to be stoic about life, to laugh at its foibles before it laughed at hers.

She gave her companion a mocking smile. "My heart always beats fast when I'm being accosted."

He stood, putting a couple of feet between them. His gaze licked over her like fire. "Accosted?" He gave a snort of laughter and his lashes dropped to dangerous levels over his eyes. "I've hardly begun. How about some lunch? The hot dogs at the bazaar looked pretty appetizing."

She blinked at the change in topic. "Why should I want to spend my time with a known criminal?"

"I paid good money for that kiss. I didn't steal it," he reminded her, his mouth turning up attractively at the corners. He thrust his hands in his back pockets and rocked back on the heels of his scuffed boots as he watched her.

"I was speaking of your assault." She stood and slipped her sandals back on. "Yes, lunch would be fine. My aunt and uncle must have heard about the kiss by now. It will reassure everyone to see me whole and well. Also, it might save you from getting beaten up by my more ardent protectors if we're seen together."

This time he blinked in confusion as she jumped from subject to subject with no pause. She grinned at him.

He lifted her left hand. "Those ardent pals of yours haven't put a ring on your finger."

"How observant of you," she murmured, pulling away and running her fingers through her hair to smooth the heavy waves into place. She felt vibrantly alive, she realized. Strong and eager for life. She cast a wary eye on her companion, wondering what it was about him that affected her so.

"Let's go." He took her arm. "Don't you lock up?" he asked when they went out on the porch.

"Not during the day. What would be the point? Everyone knows I hide the key over the door."

He gave her a sardonic glance. "Is the whole town as trusting as you?"

"I'm not trusting," she shot right back. "If thieves want anything I've got, they'll get in anyway. If the door's open, they can go right in without breaking anything. See? It's simple logic."

"I have a feeling nothing is going to be simple about our relationship."

She cast him a startled glance from under her lashes. Again a vision of the future came to her—of her running across a field with this man, holding hands and laughing, a child and a dog running ahead of them . . .

Retreating to sober reality, she realized he not only disturbed her heart, he sent her dreams into a tailspin. She didn't understand it.

"We don't have a relationship," she stated.

"We will," he declared.

2

———◄

"Would it be rude to ask your name?" Anne asked. She placed the two cups of cola on the table. The cups, one red, the other green, heralded the season's colors.

Her companion put the hot dogs and curly fries, seasoned with Tex-Mex spices, on the table beside the drinks. "Jonathan Sinclair—Jon to my friends." He smiled as if at some secret thought while he pulled out a chair and held it for her.

"Sinclair? As in Sinclair Ranch?"

"Right."

Instead of sitting, she held out her hand. "Anne Hyden, as in the Flower Garden."

He shook her hand, then held it as he asked, "Should this mean something to me?"

"I'm one of your customers. In fact, I have a big order in for Christmas. That's only a little over three weeks away," she reminded him. "It is going to be ready, isn't it?"

He had no idea. "Would I let one of my best customers down?" He sincerely hoped not. That might delay, although not impede, the relationship between them.

"It's been known to happen," she said wryly. She took her seat. He sat opposite her.

She bit into her hot dog. He did the same. She tried to keep her eyes off him, but it was difficult. He had no such qualms. He stared at her, an gleam of intrigue in his eyes, as they ate. A man to watch out for, she decided. A man who could be dangerous to a woman's heart.

"So you own a flower shop," he said when he finished.

"Yes. It was a dream come true to be able to buy it when the owner retired." She'd had to fight her aunt every step of the way, right up to the final closing. She licked a smear of mustard off her lips.

"I'd like to do that for you," he murmured, his gaze glued to her mouth.

She wiped her lips with a napkin. "You're disconcerting."

"Do I make you nervous?"

More than that. He conjured up old dreams of forbidden things as a magician conjured up a hatful of Texas-size rabbits. "Yes. You're rather unpredictable."

"I'm not dangerous . . . only fascinated."

"Do you always come on this strong?"

Jon wondered about that, too. It was unusual for him. Her forthright manner put him at ease. "Only when I know it's going to be stupendous."

"What?" She brushed her hair away from her face, another nervous gesture, he surmised.

"Our coming together." He realized that could be taken more than one way and grinned when she fidgeted with her hair. He did make her nervous. It wasn't a tenth of what she did to him. He could hardly wait to show her. But first . . .

"I'm not a marrying man," he told her bluntly and watched to see how she'd take it.

"Has anyone ever asked you?" she inquired with only a token of polite interest after the briefest of pauses.

A surprised second ticked past. He threw back his head and laughed in delight. "This is going to be fun."

"The chase or the seduction?" The imp danced in her eyes as she looked him over as an old-maid schoolmarm might.

"Both," he promised, meaning it. He hooked an arm over the chair and pushed it onto the two back legs while he watched the thoughts dart through her eyes. He wished he could read them. She was an interesting woman.

"Oh-oh," she said sotto voce. "Here come my relatives."

He glanced over his shoulder. A man in a lightweight suit, a blue shirt and striped tie came toward them. The woman beside him wore a beige lace dress. They seemed to be dressed for a formal wedding rather than a bazaar. They were around fifty, a handsome couple actually, the man a tad thin, the woman a tad plump, but both energetic and healthy-looking.

He got to his feet when they approached the table.

Anne introduced them before they could speak. "My aunt and uncle, Marge and Joseph Pauly. Uncle Joe is the mayor. Aunt Marge is on the city council. She opposed him on a land-use tax and got elected. This is Jon Sinclair."

"Marge. Joe. Glad to meet you." Jon shook hands with them. He felt like a suitor on display as they looked him over.

As on the tax issue, he realized they had assessed him and come up on opposite sides. The mayor smiled benevolently; the councilwoman smiled coldly, disapproval in her eyes—which were the same intriguing blue as her niece's.

The defiance he'd felt as a teenager surfaced. One thing he hated was being censured by self-righteous harpies, male or female.

"Are you all right?" The aunt turned to her niece as soon as the amenities were over. She peered at the younger woman so anxiously that Jon studied her, too.

She looked fine to him—a woman of many charms, all of which he'd like to sample. Also, she was levelheaded. She'd taken his announcement about marriage without a blink. Good. He liked savvy women.

"Of course," Anne replied. "Did you know that Jon has taken over the Sinclair Ranch? It supplies the mums I get in for fall and the poinsettias at Christmas. He's supplying the plants I'll need for the country club dance during Christmas week." She gave him a significant look that said those flowers had better be ready. Jon vowed to check on them first thing.

"You raise flowers?" The aunt was frankly disbelieving.

Jon assumed a broad grin and tried to look the part. "Yes, ma'am, I do, on one of the prettiest little spreads in all of Texas," he drawled.

Anne nudged him with a sharp elbow. "Laying it on too thick, Sinclair. These are astute politicians."

He tried to look subdued by her reprimand, but a smile kept blooming on his lips. He hadn't enjoyed himself this much in years. Anne was a challenge he couldn't resist.

The uncle grinned at him, but the aunt looked annoyed. Hmm, he'd have to work on the old biddy and see if he couldn't thaw her out a little. However, before he could compliment her on her dress, she turned to her niece, effectively tuning him out.

"I went by the booth. Ellen said you'd had all the kisses you could stand for one day," her aunt said anxiously.

"Snooze Allyn said you fainted." She put a hand on Anne's forehead. "I knew you shouldn't be standing around in the sun like that."

"Well, it was for a good cause." Anne beamed a smile at Jon and moved a step away from her aunt's solicitous care. "And I made almost a hundred dollars."

"Yeah, you still owe me," he reminded her.

A tiny thrill worked its way down Anne's back. His eyes issued a dare. She wished . . . "You got your kiss, cowboy."

"One. That leaves nineteen to go."

She caught her breath at the thought of nineteen more of those kisses. "I can't hold my breath that long."

"We'll take short breaks," he assured her.

Their eyes met in a duel of laughter and desire. He was a man to steal a maiden's heart, she acknowledged. Longing flowed through her like wind through a willow.

"Is Randall coming home this week?" the aunt interrupted.

"Uh, no. Not that I know of."

Silver eyes narrowed on her. "Who's Randall?" Jon asked, ignoring her aunt and uncle, both of whom listened in on the conversation with blatant interest.

"The senator from our district," Anne replied. "He's in Austin while the state legislature is in session."

"Oh, a politician."

With these words and a casual shrug, the senator was dismissed as being unimportant in her life. "Yes. We see each other." She waited for Jon's reaction to this statement.

"As in exclusively?" he demanded, his gaze spearing into hers, thrilling her with his quick concern.

"Really," Aunt Marge said indignantly. "It's hardly any of *your* business."

He shoved his hat off his forehead, stuck his hands in his rear pockets and rocked back on his heels. A posture he assumed when he was considering things, Anne decided, remembering his doing the same at her house.

The action pulled his jeans snug across his lean hips. She recalled the feel of his hard body against hers when she'd fallen against him at the kissing booth. He'd been aroused.

Heat surged through her in tiny star bursts of reaction to his masculine stance. She was attracted to him . . . in a way she'd never been to Randall. Her heart had never gone out of control when the handsome politician kissed her. It was worrisome.

Did she dare take Jon Sinclair on as an opponent? He'd made it clear he was looking for adventure. Was she? One mad adventure before eternity closed over her?

"Would you care to join us?" he asked her aunt and uncle. "I'll be glad to get you a hot dog or whatever you like."

A polite maverick. She gave him a smile of approval.

"We've had lunch, but a tall, cool lemonade would taste real good right now," the uncle spoke up.

Jon noted the mayor's Texas drawl had thickened a bit. When he glanced that way, the mayor smiled. Jon thought he saw an imp of mischief in Joe's dark brown eyes. Uncle and niece shared the same sense of humor.

"Yes, that would be nice," Marge said, her gaze darting from Anne to him. "I'll help you get them."

Jon raised one eyebrow but followed along at the woman's heels as she led the way across the lawn. As soon as they were out of hearing of the other two, she turned on him in squinty-eyed disapproval.

"Anne has a heart condition," she told him in a low, intense tone. "She mustn't be upset in any way."

This wasn't what he'd expected to hear. He glanced over his shoulder. Anne looked the picture of health to him—pink cheeks, clear eyes, a smiling mouth, a firm, luscious body. His heart kicked up at the thought...as well as other parts.

Was this warning some kind of ploy on the aunt's part? She didn't exactly keep it a secret that she favored the senator as the companion of choice for her niece. But that was for Anne to decide. She was a mature adult.

He spread his hands in an innocent gesture. "I wouldn't think of upsetting Anne."

"This isn't funny, Mr. Sinclair."

"I'm not laughing." He leveled a steady gaze on her as the old rebellious spirit stirred in him. Being told not to do something had always set him on a direct path for it. Of course, rebellion sometimes led to disaster.

"Just what are your intentions toward my niece?" the older woman demanded, stopping in the shade of the oak tree and out of sight of the other two.

He gave her a cool glance. "I think that's between Anne and me. She is of age, isn't she?"

"She's twenty-five. And a virgin."

"I'm thirty-one. And I'm not."

Ignoring her indignant gasp, he headed for the lemonade stand and ordered four drinks. The gorgon gave him the silent treatment on the return trip. Which was okay by him.

Anne glanced from one expressionless face to the other. She sighed dramatically. "My aunt give you the medical diagnosis?"

"Yes," Jon admitted, looking her over.

"Still planning to seduce me?" she asked, mostly out of curiosity. Men fled when they found out she might turn into a liability rather than a lover.

"Anne!" her aunt admonished.

"Yes," Jon said, meeting her eyes. He grinned.

Anne placed a final spray of greenery in a bouquet of yellow and pink roses, then stepped back and eyed the arrangement. She nodded in satisfaction at its loveliness.

Doc Adamson had ordered an impressive array of flowers for his cousin's thirty-ninth birthday. Ellen Adamson had directed his office and business affairs for the past two years with cheerful efficiency, but this was the first time he'd sent her flowers. Perhaps this signified a change in their relationship.

For a tenth of a second, Anne was wistful, then she pushed aside the feeling. If she ever married, it would be to a man like Randall, someone who wouldn't expect too much from her.

Her aunt and uncle liked him and had encouraged their dating. Randall had hinted several times of late that he wanted to ask for more from her, but she'd managed to evade the final question. She wasn't quite ready to commit herself....

A restlessness stirred in her, a longing for something more. *Excitement. Danger. Romance.* Oh, sure.

She shouldn't expect fireworks, rainbows and all that. She knew wild romance was only in books and movies. Still, she wondered about it sometimes. A startling thought came to her— Jon Sinclair could give her all those.

But then, what about commitment and mutual respect and common goals? Excitement and danger were childish fantasies. And wild romance was not lasting devotion. Randall was a much better choice. If she ever decided to marry.

Another wild idea intruded. Wasn't a person entitled to one mad fling before settling down to marital and family bliss and responsibility?

She was shocked at the errant ways of her mind. She had always been the soul of respectability. After all, Randall had two sons—one in his first year of college and one a junior in high school who still lived at home. She liked the boys and would be a model parent for them. If she married.

The bell tinkled over the door, announcing a customer.

She stuck her head around the corner. "Ellen, hi," she called, seeing her friend. "Be right with you." She quickly hid the bouquet with a covering of colorful foil paper and walked into the front part of the flower shop.

"I thought I'd see if you had time for coffee," Ellen Adamson said, admiring a wreath made of Christmas bows with cinnamon sticks and sachets of cloves to add a holiday scent. Monday was the day the doctor did routine surgery. The office was closed, and so Ellen had the day pretty much to herself.

"Give me a second to freshen up." Anne renewed her lipstick and checked her hair. She wore it clipped out of the way with a big bow at the back of her neck while she worked. "Okay, let's go." She stuck a Be Back Soon sign in the window.

The two friends walked two doors down the block to a restaurant and took a free table amid a myriad of hanging plants. Anne picked a couple of dead leaves off a spider plant and checked its moisture level before taking her seat.

"That was some kiss Saturday," Ellen commented after the waitress had departed with their order.

"Yes." Anne tried for a nonchalant manner and failed.

"I was coming to rescue you, but you fainted before I got there. Quick thinking, that."

Anne cleared her throat. "Thanks, but it wasn't all an act. I sort of panicked, then things went dark. When I realized what had happened, I decided to go along with it. I was afraid my aunt would club him if she saw him kissing me like that."

"A couple of guys were ready to step in when you made your dramatic move. I was worried about you for a minute."

"You were?"

"Mmm-hmm. Until I saw your face." Ellen laughed softly. "You looked totally blissed-out. Was the kiss that wonderful?"

Anne hesitated. "Yes."

"Oh." Ellen studied her a second. "That sounded like a very serious yes."

Anne lifted the bangs off her forehead. "Is it suddenly hot in here or am I blushing?"

"Blushing. This gets more interesting by the minute. What are you going to do about Jon Sinclair?"

"I don't know," she hedged. "Got any advice?" She wasn't sure if she should confess, even to her best friend, the insane idea that kept occurring to her.

"Go for it," Ellen announced.

"Go for it?"

"Right."

Anne frowned at her friend. "Are we talking about the same thing?"

"I hope so. I think you should have a torrid, tempestuous affair, one that will singe your eyebrows."

Anne had to laugh. "That kiss nearly did."

Ellen became serious. "I don't want to see you settle for... oh, I don't know, less than you deserve. Randall is almost twenty years older than you."

"Does that matter?"

"Maybe. Everyone deserves that wild, impossibly insane first love. I'd hate to see you miss out on it."

Anne watched Ellen become pensive, her smile bittersweet. Her friend had once been married, but it hadn't worked out.

"Everyone should have that first sweet taste of passion," Ellen continued. "For men, it's called sowing their wild oats. For women, it's gather ye rosebuds while ye may."

"This advice from a doctor's right-hand person? What about safe sex and all that?"

"I didn't say not to be careful. Just have fun while you're doing it."

"Jon Sinclair told me he wasn't a marrying man."

Shock momentarily stopped Ellen, then she grinned in pure glee. "Arrogant beast," she murmured. "So it has already gotten that far." She gave Anne a purely speculative perusal. "From a kiss to talk of marriage in one breath. Impressive. You must have singed more than his eyebrows."

Anne lowered her lashes demurely and murmured wickedly, "I hope so. I like to give as well as I get."

Ellen looked momentarily disconcerted at this statement. "Can this be the Anne Hyden we've come to know and love?" she questioned, then she chortled. "Oh, this is going to be good," she declared, clearly seeing the affair as the coming event.

Anne was tempted. "One passionate affair before settling into domestic bliss?" she mused, unable to keep from thinking about that wild, erotic caress.

"Bliss? Or boredom?"

"I'm very fond of Randall," she said firmly.

"I'm fond of my dog, but I wouldn't care to depend on him for witty conversation. Have you ever thought of being alone with Randall for days on end if, for instance, you were stranded on a desert island for a month?''

"Well, no."

A picture came to Anne. Jon Sinclair, dressed in ragged cutoffs, his body lean and bronzed by the sun, standing ankle-deep in the ocean, homemade spear lifted to catch their dinner.

"So how does Jon Sinclair look standing on a deserted beach?" Ellen's snicker broke into Anne's musing.

"You're putting ideas in my head," Anne told her.

"It's time someone did. I think Marge tried to make an old maid out of you from the day you were born."

It was no secret the two women didn't get along. Ellen thought Marge was too possessive and overprotective of Anne. Marge thought Ellen was a bad influence.

Anne thought her aunt's attitude was because Marge had been there when Anne's mother had died in childbirth. Uncle Joe and Aunt Marge had raised her from the time she was a toddler because her father traveled extensively in his job with an international corporation. He hadn't been home in almost two years.

Aunt Marge meant well. She, too, had been affected by the family curse—two children had died in infancy from heart defects. Anne loved her aunt and tried not to resent the older woman's interference in her life. Aunt Marge reminded her to be careful because she was concerned about Anne's health.

Thinking of her reaction to the kiss, Anne shook her head ruefully. "I'm not sure my heart is up to an affair with Jon Sinclair."

"But you won't know until you try."

"Have you ever had an affair?"

Ellen was silent so long, Anne thought she wasn't going to answer. "Once. A long time ago."

"Did it make your heart pound like it would fly right out of your chest?"

"Of course. That's the point of the whole thing."

Their coffee and muffins arrived. Anne changed the subject, but the memory of the kiss lingered in her mind. It stayed in the minds of her neighbors, too. Before Anne had finished her coffee, five people drifted over and asked if she was feeling better.

"It is the biggest raisin on the grapevine, or something like that," Ellen advised when Anne grumbled about the avid interest in her love life.

Jon Sinclair kicked the sheet off and swung out of bed. Naked, he walked to the window and looked out at the dawn. From his bedroom, located on the second floor of the sprawling home of his youth, he could see the Sabine River chugging along on its way to the Gulf of Mexico.

He was restless and hungry. But not for food. Glancing down, he shook his head in wry exasperation. His body was erect and ready for a torrid session between the sheets.

The emptiness of his bed only underscored the problem. Last night, eating a lonely supper in a seafood place along the river, he'd passed up the chance to spend a few pleasant hours in another bed.

Wrong woman, wrong bed.

Truth was, he couldn't get Anne Hyden out of his mind. She lingered like the annoying line of a song that wouldn't go away. It was driving him crazy.

Frowning at his own stupidity, he dressed, ate a slice of bologna stuffed into a hot-dog bun and took his coffee to the field with him. He worked on the irrigation system until Pedro, Jon's ranch manager, and his son arrived; then he left them putting PVC pipe together and went to town for more parts.

The first person he saw was Anne Hyden, looking like a perky pansy in a gold top and brown slacks. Her hair was clipped at the back of her neck with a fluffy gold bow. She was unlocking her shop door when she spied him. She stopped at the door and waved.

Her action surprised him. He'd thought she would be cool and standoffish for some reason.

He parked and jumped down from the pickup. Going to her, he nodded toward the restaurant. "How about some breakfast?"

"I've eaten." The dimples winked saucily at him.

He thought of crushing them under his lips. "Then you can watch me while I eat."

"Okay."

Again, he was thrown slightly off-balance. She never reacted the way he thought she would. When she fell into step beside him, he took her hand and swung it between them.

"I've dreamed of you for two nights now," he complained, giving her an oblique glance to see how she took this statement.

"Oh, too bad." She laughed when he frowned at her.

A grin came over him in spite of his irritation at her cavalier attitude toward his sleepless nights. "You're driving me up the wall," he announced, guiding her into the restaurant.

"This your new office?" the waitress asked Anne when they were seated. The woman gave him a speculative glance.

"It looks that way." Anne gave an attractive shrug. "I'll have tea this time."

Jon ordered the waffle special. When the waitress left, he asked Anne, "You've already been in this morning, I take it?"

She nodded. "Ellen Adamson and I were in earlier. We were discussing you."

"Who's Ellen Adamson?" He searched his memory for a face and came up blank.

"Doc Adamson's cousin. She was the one who pointed out my house Saturday and kept things calm while you made your getaway."

"Ah, yes. Is she a nurse?"

"No, but she runs his office. He hired her about two years ago, shortly after his wife died in a car crash. Ellen and Doc grew up here. As a teenager Ellen used to baby-sit me. When she returned to town as an adult, we became the best of friends."

Their coffee and tea arrived. He scorned the sugar and cream and watched while Anne added both to her tea. He noted the way her fingers curled around the handle of the cup when she lifted it to her mouth and sipped cautiously in case it was too hot. Her dimples appeared when she grinned at him.

"Not going to ask, huh?" she said.

"Ask what?"

"What Ellen and I were saying about you."

"I've never much cared what people said about me." He took a drink of coffee and found it hot and strong.

"She thinks we should have an affair."

He nearly spewed the coffee on the table, but managed to swallow it instead. Then he choked.

She patted him on the back and made sympathetic noises.

"What did you think?" he asked as soon as he was able.

"It sounded…interesting." The imp of mischief peeked at him from her blue-violet eyes.

"How interesting?"

"Make me an offer."

"Dinner tonight. My place."

She shook her head. "Too easy. You'll have to court me first, I think. Candlelight and romance... sweet nothings in my ear and all that."

He muttered an expletive. The expressive eyebrows went up as she studied him, a slight smile lingering on her mouth.

"If it's too much trouble..." Her voice trailed off as she gazed at him.

"I'll walk over coals," he told her bluntly. "I just hoped I wouldn't have to."

His meal arrived—waffle, bacon, two eggs over-medium and an assortment of attractively arranged orange and cantaloupe slices.

"But the chase makes the end that much sweeter, don't you think?" She was all wide-eyed innocence.

"I think you're going to make me run till I drop," he muttered darkly. He dashed pepper vigorously on his eggs before chopping them into pieces. He gave her a challenging glance as he lifted a bite to his mouth. "However, the race isn't over until someone crosses the finish line. That'll be me."

He grinned and started eating.

There was nothing arrogant about his confidence, Anne noted. He was quietly sure he would win this chase... battle... whatever... between them. Maybe they both would.

"There won't be a loser," he added in a husky tone, reading her mind. "I'll take you over the line with me."

"Mmm," she said noncommittally.

"Your aunt said you were a virgin."

Anne shook her head in exasperation. "How could she presume to know that?"

"You're not saying, huh?" His gaze was speculative . . . and a little troubled.

"I was almost engaged once. In college." she told him in a low voice as the waitress brought fresh coffee.

"I see."

He didn't ask her about what had happened. She wasn't going to confess that the relationship hadn't gone beyond a few torrid kisses, none of which had made her feel more than slightly breathless. She glanced at Jon's mouth and wondered what kind of magic he'd used on her and if she'd feel it again if they kissed.

The waitress leaned over him as she refilled his coffee cup, her arm brushing his as she did. There was a wealth of invitation in the action. Anne found it irritating.

With something akin to shock, she realized she was jealous. "I need to get back to the shop. I have several orders to fill for delivery this afternoon."

"I'll walk you back."

"Stay and finish your coffee while it's hot." She stood.

So did he. He seemed tall and powerful. "If you're leaving, I'm finished," he told her.

"A very diplomatic way of putting it."

"And true." He laid a bill on the table and took her hand as they left.

At the flower shop, he went inside and looked around. "Very nice," he commented, sniffing a bouquet.

He followed her when she stored her purse on a shelf in her workroom. Suddenly he was very close.

Her eyes went wide when she saw the intent in his eyes. "I don't think—"

"Good," he murmured. He slipped his arms behind her and gathered her close.

With a sigh, she leaned into his embrace. Wrapping her arms around his neck, she lifted her face, closed her eyes and waited for his kiss...and waited...and waited.

She opened her eyes. He was watching her.

"Yes?" she said, flustered by his stare.

"Do you want the sweet nothings now or later?" he inquired politely, a hint of a smile in his eyes.

It took less than a second to decide. "Later." She pulled his head down to hers, surprised at the urgency.

"I like aggressive women," he murmured.

She shut him up by the simple expedient of rising on tiptoe and pressing her lips to his. She felt his breath catch, then a shudder ripple through his lean frame.

His hands traveled a restless circuit over her back, again and again. She felt surrounded by his male presence and sensed the power he held in check. Perhaps this wasn't wise....

"Open your mouth," he whispered against her lips.

"I don't like openmouthed kisses," she tried to explain, then remembered how exciting it had felt to run her tongue over his lips when he'd kissed her at the bazaar.

"That was before," he muttered.

"Yes," she agreed.

He deepened the kiss before she could protest, his tongue sliding easily between her parted lips and dipping into her mouth as if he were tasting honey.

She became lost in the sensuous feelings he aroused in her. Instinctively she moved against the hard ridge that pressed so provocatively against her. The knowledge of his arousal fed her own excitement. She felt his hands slide down her back and cup her buttocks, bringing her into closer contact.

With a gasp, she threaded her fingers into his dark hair and pulled him closer. The kiss became hungrier, more demanding.

He pressed her against the wall, holding her there with his strength while his hands roamed over her. Finally he stopped his roaming and settled both hands over her breasts, taking their weight in his palms, then rubbing the tips with his thumbs until both stood out against her knit top.

The dizziness she'd experienced on Saturday returned. No! She didn't want to faint and miss a second of this bliss.

The bell jingled over the front door.

"Hello. Anybody home?" someone called.

With an effort, she brought her senses under control. Her companion didn't seem to notice the interruption. She twisted her face to the side. He caught a handful of her hair and buried his face against the side of her neck, holding her captive while he controlled his breathing.

"Be . . . be with you in a minute," Anne called. "I'm . . . uh . . . tied up at the moment."

"It's the mail. I'll put it on the counter."

"Oh, yes . . . thanks." She could hardly pull a coherent word from her dazed mind.

"See you tomorrow." The bell jingled again.

Silence pervaded the shop.

"Is she gone?" Jon murmured against her neck.

"Yes."

He took several deep breaths and lifted his head. His gaze searched hers in a somber manner. "That's the second time this has happened to me."

"What?"

"Forgetting everything because of you."

Her own reactions to his nearness were more primitive and lustful than anything she'd ever felt. "I know."

He released her slowly, reluctantly. "The invitation to dinner still stands."

"Maybe we'd better think on that," she suggested, troubled by the way her body went haywire when he touched her.

It occurred to her that her aunt might be right. Maybe her heart couldn't handle this kind of intense excitement. It seemed so unfair—to find ecstasy and not be able to savor it. Her entire life had been like that, and she wanted more...*more*...

"Yeah," he agreed. He stepped back and looked down.

Her gaze followed his. He was still rigid with desire. Heat swept through her again, making her weak with longing. She wasn't sure she liked another person having this much power over her. It seemed too serious for an affair.

He recovered his equilibrium first, and his sense of humor. "Eighteen to go," he told her with a wry chuckle and headed for the front door.

"That surely counted for more than one," she protested.

She followed him, smoothing her knit shirt over her slacks. She couldn't help but note that his shirt was half out of his jeans. She'd done that, pulling at it, wanting it out of the way so she could touch his bare skin.

He turned at the door. "No way." His gaze caressed her before he left. "When will I see you?"

Alone and uninterrupted was the rest of the sentence.

"I don't know."

"Scared?" he challenged.

"Yes."

"Me, too."

She stared into his eyes. Then, for some reason that escaped her, they both smiled. He nodded briefly as if making his mind up to some silent concern, then left.

She leaned against the wall, a hand pressed to the pounding ache in her chest, and wondered how to let go once a person caught a tiger by the tail.

...

3

Jon stood on the sidewalk beside his truck. He checked his watch, then frowned at the building. The receptionist had said the office closed at five on Thursdays. The last patient had left thirty minutes ago. Where was Ellen Adamson?

"Hello. What are you doing here?"

He spun around. Ellen came toward him from a side door of the medical building. She stopped where the two sidewalks joined and smiled at him. Her eyes held a question.

"You got a minute?" he asked. "I'd like to talk to you." He stuck his hands in his back pockets. "I thought we might go have a bite to eat. If you're free."

She hesitated, then nodded. "The diner?"

"Sure."

He fell into step beside her, unable to think of a single item of small talk. "About Anne," he began hesitantly.

"Now, why did I think her name might come up in this conversation?" Ellen asked. Her expression was kind.

"Yeah, well, I have some questions." He held open the door to the small restaurant, then followed Ellen inside. She chose a table in a secluded corner. The waitress brought them menus and water right away. They waited until she left.

"Sweep her off her feet," Ellen said.

"What?" He surely wasn't hearing correctly.

"Sweep Anne off her feet," she explained with a patient air. "She deserves some fun in her life...for a change."

Jon frowned. "I'm not planning on staying here."

"Why not? It's a nice place to raise a family. Richport was your home once. It's time you were settling down."

"Spoken like a true female."

His companion ignored the sardonic statement. "Anyway, it doesn't matter. I want Anne to have one glorious experience in her life before she succumbs to boredom."

He took a sip of water to douse the fire her advice incited and to gain some time, then decided he'd better come right out with it. "Her aunt told me Anne has a heart condition."

Ellen nodded.

"Is it safe for her...I mean, if... How serious is it?"

Understanding dawned in the brown eyes watching him as if she could see right into his mind. He tried to block the memory of the kisses he and Anne had shared—two of them, so potent, the thought made him burn with longing.

"It's nothing to worry about," Ellen assured him in a soft voice. "Certainly it's nothing that would preclude a normal relationship between a man and a woman."

He heard the slight stress on *normal,* but it didn't relieve his worries. "She fainted in my arms last Saturday although she pretended afterward that it was an act. Part of it was real, I think. And her heart beats so hard when I touch her..."

The thought trailed away as he recalled how she'd felt in his arms. She became as lost in their kisses as he did.

"What else would you expect with an aunt like Marge?" Ellen demanded, her eyes narrowing in anger.

"Explain that."

Ellen sighed in disgust. "All her life Anne's been told she mustn't run, she mustn't get excited, she mustn't get overheated. She wasn't allowed to participate in sports or any rough play. It's a miracle that she ever broke free and made a life for herself at all. But she did, and it's a nice one. She's happy, productive and busy. She's even thinking of marriage."

Jon scowled. "The senator may be okay, but he's not the one for Anne. She's not in love with him."

"Right. But she is thinking of marrying him. Then she meets a man who makes her feel things she's never felt before." Ellen smiled. "You've shaken her up. I personally think that's what she needs."

"What exactly is wrong with her heart?"

"She has a valve that sags a bit. If it gets to leaking, she might need a new one, but there's no indication of that happening. She can lead a perfectly ordinary life."

He gave her a skeptical glance. "Anne couldn't fake the way her heart beats when we kiss."

"If a person has been cautioned about her heart all her life, what do you think is going to happen when she runs into her first real experience with sexual excitement? It's going to be a bit overwhelming, don't you think?"

"Yeah, I see what you mean," Jon said, mulling this over. "So making love would be no danger to her?" He felt the heat sneak into his face at this disclosure.

"Making love never hurt anyone. Except for Type A middle-aged men trying to recover their lost youth," Ellen added in her usual dry manner. "I hope you won't let it put you off Anne. She needs someone to open her eyes to the things she's missed. Even if you offer nothing more than a torrid affair, at least she'll know what to look for next time. She's a first-class person. I don't want her to settle for a second-best love.''

Jon found that the idea of someone else with Anne, making love, sharing her laughter and those incredible kisses, didn't set well with him. He grimaced. Next thing he knew, he'd be dreaming of rose-covered cottages and the patter of little feet.

"Thanks for leveling with me," he said. "I don't want to hurt Anne, in spite of what Esmeralda thinks."

"Esmeralda?" Ellen questioned.

"Aunt Marge." He grinned wickedly, already gearing up for battle with the old witch.

Ellen laughed in delight. "Oh, I wouldn't miss this for the world." She studied him for a second, then added softly, "You're a fool if you let Anne get away."

"I'm not a marrying man," he informed her.

She was still laughing when the waitress came for their order. He had to grin. She didn't say it, but he had to admit it sounded like a case of him protesting too much.

One thing he knew—he'd never spent this much time worrying about whether he'd be good for a woman. In fact, he'd never thought about a relationship in those terms at all. Until Anne.

Anne sat at the table by the door, ticking off names as people arrived for the chamber of commerce dinner, which was the first Friday of each month. Their guest speaker, a professor from the university at Austin, had called in sick. Randall Talbert had agreed to come down in his place.

She could hear Randall's pleasant voice and deep chuckle behind her as he talked to the members who had already arrived. When he'd called to chat earlier that day, she'd mentioned the problem. He'd immediately volunteered to come to their aid, rearranging his schedule to do so.

"Good evening," a masculine baritone broke into her musing.

She stared up into eyes that reminded her of the river with an early-morning fog rising from its smoky surface.

Jon was dressed in a tailored suit of salt-and-pepper gray with a thread of blue running through the material. His shirt was light blue, his tie navy with a red-and-gray abstract design.

From the stubborn waves of his neatly combed black hair to the shiny toes of his wing-tip dress shoes, he looked like the successful tycoon—polished, urbane and totally at home in any situation, including a boardroom. She was impressed.

His eyes ran over her, taking in the white sheath, the jacket with the red embroidered flowers, the red bow that held her hair back out of her face. Her insides went to jelly.

"Your hair is fine," he said.

She realized she was brushing back strands of hair over her temple. She dropped her hand and went over the list. Jon Sinclair made her nervous, excited. She'd have to be wary.

"I don't see your name. Did you make a reservation?" She knew very well that he hadn't.

"Your uncle said it was okay to pay at the door when I talked to him earlier today."

"Oh. Where did you see him?"

"At the bank. He said your senator was going to be the speaker. I thought I'd drop by and look over the competition."

She smiled while her heart went into overdrive. Her aunt had called every day that week to remind her of her "condition," but surely one fling wouldn't hurt....

He paid the price of the dinner, then waited while she added his name to the roster and made out the receipt.

He caught her hand when she handed the piece of paper over. "Where are you sitting?"

"I haven't chosen a seat yet." She unobtrusively tried to withdraw her hand. He tightened his clasp.

"Good. I'll save you a place next to me. Or are you promised to someone else?"

"Well, no." Usually she sat by Randall, but since he'd be sitting at the head table as guest speaker, she was free to sit where she pleased. However, she wasn't sure she wanted that place to be next to Jon Sinclair.

He nodded cordially, released her hand and ambled off toward her uncle and Randall as if she'd agreed to sit with him. She frowned at his presumption, but she couldn't tear her eyes from his handsome profile as he was introduced to the other men by her uncle. Jon was the youngest among them, she realized.

She watched as he laughed and talked to Randall with the easy assurance of old friends.

When it was time to take their seats, Randall came over to her. "I'm to sit at the speaker's table, I understand. Are you going to sit with me?"

"Well, no. It's full already." She felt a tiny bit guilty when he grimaced in disappointment. "Come by the house after the meeting. We'll have coffee and cherry pie," she offered.

Randall's ready smile flashed over his face, deepening the lines at the corners of his mouth. Other lines fanned out from his eyes in an attractive manner. "Great."

She was rather taken aback to note how gray his hair was. While she'd admired his high, patrician forehead in the past, now she found herself wondering if it was due to a receding hairline.

A frown etched its way between her eyes. She knew where these traitorous thoughts had come from. Hearing Jon's deep, hearty laugh, she glanced at him over Randall's shoulder.

His teeth were white against the tan of his face. She remembered his neck and torso had also been brown and wondered if he went without a shirt while working in the sun.

For a second, a rush of emotion poured over her as she thought of how he would feel, all sun-warmed and sweaty from his toil, to her wandering hands. She could almost taste the salt on his skin....

"What?" She looked at Randall blankly. "I'm sorry. What did you say?"

"I was wondering if Sinclair would settle down here. A man usually comes home when he gets ready to start his family."

A family. She skidded past the thought. "Oh? Is this something you learned in Psych 101?"

Randall chuckled. "An observation on life, my dear," he replied, turning to watch Jon. "He would be good for the state and the community. He's a shrewd businessman. If I ever become governor, I want him on my team."

"Why?"

"I've talked to people who have worked with him. He's taken over a dozen companies in the last thirteen years and turned them around, changing them from losers into money-makers, then he sells them and starts over. He likes a challenge." Randall turned back to her. "God knows government provides more of that than any one person can usually handle."

"My aunt and uncle would agree." Anne studied Jon in his dress clothes. "So he's made a success of himself since he left home," she mused. "I thought he only had the ranch."

"That's the very least of his holdings."

"You talking about the Sinclair boy?" Doc Adamson strolled in, the very last as usual.

"Hello, Doc. Yes, we were discussing his success in the business world," Randall explained.

"He's sharp, that one," Doc agreed. "I remember he was kind of wild in his young days. The town bad boy, some called him, but he was just full of high spirits and pranks." Doc shook his head. "That Skaggs girl nearly caught him, though."

"How?" Anne demanded, unpleasantly surprised by this news.

"She said he got her in the family way, but he told me he never touched her."

"Did you believe him?" she asked, unable to hide her interest in the case.

"Yes," Doc said good-naturedly. "Young Sinclair said he'd take care of the child if blood tests proved it was his. The girl confessed the truth when she saw she couldn't force him to the altar. It turned out the baby belonged to her daddy's hired hand. She was scared her old man would shoot the boyfriend if he found out. She knew he wouldn't harm a Sinclair."

"Close call," Randall said in male sympathy.

Anne breathed a sigh of relief. She signed in the doctor, smiled at Randall when he left to take his seat and wrote a check to the restaurant for the number of meals to be served.

When everything was accounted for, she stole quietly to the table where Jon sat while the president of the group read off a list of announcements. Jon pulled her chair out and seated her in a gallant fashion.

"Thank you," she whispered.

"My pleasure."

The announcements were finished and dinner began.

Jon's gaze roamed over her as she picked up the salad fork. "You look good enough to eat in that outfit. Red is your color."

"Most people think blue is. Because of my eyes," she added when he shook his head.

"You're much too passionate for blue. No," he mused, gazing at her as if making a weighty decision. "Red is it."

She gave him a quelling glance. "You'd better eat. We have to move right along with the program in order to be out on time."

He poured a vinegar-and-oil dressing on his greens and started eating. "Your senator seems like a nice guy."

"Yes, he is."

"Doesn't it bother you that you'll be cheating him?"

That brought her head around. She tried a freezing stare. "Whatever are you talking about?"

"A husband expects a bit a passion from his wife. Are you going to let him see that side of you?"

She could feel the blood racing toward her face... and other parts of her body. "Of course."

"You haven't so far," Jon reminded her. He flicked a knowing glance at the head table and back at her.

"How do you know that?" she demanded.

"Because men and women who are intimate invade each other's space without even realizing it. You and the senator don't."

Anne marveled at his insight. She'd noted that her married friends often touched each other affectionately, but she hadn't really thought about why. Of course they were comfortable in touching each other. After the intimacy of the bed, anything else had to be considered casual.

He ate in silence for a few minutes, until after the waiter had removed their plates and set the main course in front of them.

"Chicken," he said.

"Don't you like chicken?" she asked.

A slow grin spread over his face. "When I first struck out on my own, after working as a bouncer in a bar for four months—until two brothers, each about the size of a bull elephant, laid me out on the floor—I took a job at a chicken factory. I almost became a vegetarian after that."

She laughed at his droll grimace.

"But I learned a lot about raising and dressing chickens," he confessed.

"Was that the first company you turned around and put in the black?"

He didn't answer for a minute. "How do you know about that?" he asked finally.

"Randall told me. He said if he were governor, he'd want you on his team."

"Government? No way. The thought of all that red tape makes me think of lynchings and things like that."

"So tell me about these companies you saved."

"There's not much to tell."

"Spoken like a true hero," she teased. "So the chicken factory was the first? Did you buy it?"

"Nah, I got mad and told the owner how the place should be run one day. He told me to go at it. I did. Eight months later, he gave me a bonus. A year later, he gave me a slice of the company for my own. We sold it to Tyson Foods for a tidy profit the year after that. That was my first experience with capitalism. I learned a lot."

"Such as?" She cut a bite of chicken and ate it while they talked. The meat was tender and tasty.

"Watch your back. Know who the competition is, inside and outside the company."

"Let's see, a longtime employee was jealous of your success and tried to do you in," she deduced. "Did he sell your secrets to a rival chicken factory?"

He tapped her on the temple with a finger. "You're damned sharp. It was the boss's nephew. He got worried about his position and tried to sabotage our operations."

"But you discovered his nefarious scheme and stopped him," she concluded.

He nodded. "But I learned a lesson."

"What?"

"Don't get between family. It's a dangerous position for outsiders. They always lose."

"Did you?" She was prying shamelessly, but he didn't seem to mind her curiosity.

"In a way. The boss's daughter and I were...seeing each other. She believed her cousin when he said I was selling out the company—"

"How?"

Jon frowned at his own disclosures. He hadn't talked this much about himself in the past ten years and here he was, spilling his guts to a woman he hardly knew.

Except he felt he did know her. As if she were the other half of his soul.

The idea was startling. He wasn't a romantic, and it was definitely a romantic notion—sweet, idealistic and stupid. "He said my tactics would bankrupt the business, laying it open for a takeover by a stronger company."

"But instead you made it a success."

She beamed approval at him. His heart did strange things in his chest—frolicking about like a spring lamb in a meadow. That was as odd as the idea that she was part of his soul.

When the meal was finished, a dessert of sorbet was served and the speaker introduced. In talking to Anne, Jon realized he'd forgotten about the older man being present. He wondered if she'd forgotten, too.

They applauded politely when Randall rose to address the audience. Jon's leg brushed Anne's as he shifted to a more comfortable position. He wanted to touch her, he discovered. It was an overpowering urge.

Her left hand was lying in her lap. He reached over and took it in his. She gave him a startled glance, then looked back toward the front. When she tried to shake him off, he held on, lacing his fingers through hers.

She looked so vital, he found it hard to believe she had a heart problem at all. It didn't stop him from wanting her, but he'd go easy with her. Their lovemaking would be gentle. . . .

He tightened his hold on her. Her hand was smaller and softer than his, but there was also strength in it. He resisted the urge to explore further for about two minutes, then he pressed her hand against his thigh and released it.

Anne tried to keep her attention focused on Randall's speech, but it was hopeless. When Jon released her hand, she didn't know whether she felt relief or disappointment. Before she could discreetly withdraw it into her own lap again, he touched her, this time drawing his fingertips along her palm, out to her fingertips and back.

He explored each small callus at the base of her fingers, then outlined her fingers against his thigh, drawing his index finger languidly around each one, pausing to stroke the tips with loverlike thoroughness once in a while.

Heat gathered in her hand and flowed up her arm until it suffused her whole body in a rosy glow. With a start, she realized he was subtly making love to her through her hand . . . and she was letting him.

She looked at him, her eyes wide, questioning. He smiled warmly, sexily at her, and laid his hand flat on hers, moving it slightly to increase and decrease the pressure. Her breath caught. She forced herself to exhale slowly and silently.

The laughter of the others around her made her jump. Jon tightened his hand on hers.

Glancing around, she saw the men at their table were engrossed in Randall's talk. She frowned at Jon. She needed to concentrate. Randall always wanted her opinion afterward, and she couldn't even remember the topic he'd chosen.

When Jon refused to let go, she pushed her thumbnail against the back of his hand, warning him she would dig in if he didn't release her. He didn't.

She found she couldn't bring herself to actually take a chance of hurting him.

He gazed at her. Ripples of alarm ran through her at the expression in his eyes. There was desire, yes, but tenderness, too. It completely unnerved her. She could only stare into his eyes, trapped by feelings too turbulent to name.

Applause brought her to her senses. She jerked her hand free and clapped vigorously with the rest of the crowd at the end of the speech. Jon did the same.

Anne fled to Randall's side, needing his calming presence to bring her back to reality. Standing by him as he shook hands with the departing guests, she met Jon's amused gaze with greater equanimity than she felt.

"Great talk," he said to Randall when he came abreast of them. "You're surely thinking of heading for Washington."

"Perhaps," Randall admitted, "but not until my youngest son graduates from high school. Family comes first, you know."

"Don't I ever," Jon agreed with a wry twist to his smile.

Anne was reminded of the woman who'd believed her wicked cousin over Jon and so had lost him. As she deserved to do.

"How about a cup of coffee?"

It took Anne a moment to realize Jon was talking to her. "Oh, no, I can't. I have plans."

"Say, I'd like to talk to you," Randall told Jon, then turned to Anne. "Got another piece of that cherry pie for Sinclair?"

"Of course." She did the polite thing. "Please, won't you join us?"

"Sure. Thanks."

She didn't trust that innocent smile for a minute. However, Jon and the senator hit it off well at her house. They launched into a discussion of the political scene while she made coffee and sliced the pie she'd baked that afternoon when she knew Randall was coming down.

"How's Sean?" she asked, returning to the living room with the tray. Jon leapt to his feet to help her.

"Fine," Randall replied. "He said to tell you his pitching has improved since you were there last."

She laughed, remembering the ball whacking her on the head when she was catching a few tosses for him. Randall's attractive chuckle joined in. Jon smiled and glanced from one to the other. She realized he felt left out.

It caused a funny feeling to invade her insides. She didn't like him being an outsider. She quickly explained the incident before speaking to Randall again. "Tell Sean it was my poor catching that was to blame."

"I will." Randall looked at his watch, then at Jon. He settled back against the sofa. She realized he was determined to wait out the younger man.

Nervous about the outcome of the evening, she gathered the dishes and loaded the tray. "I'll bring some more coffee," she murmured, lifting the tray.

Strong hands took it from her. "I'll help."

She let Jon take the tray to the kitchen. "Just set it on the counter there." She picked up the coffeepot.

He lingered. "I'll rinse these and put them in the dishwasher for you."

Nodding, she returned to the living room, poured more coffee and headed back for the kitchen to see if he was really doing the dishes. He was.

She replaced the coffeepot, then leaned against the counter while she watched him finish. "Here's a towel." She handed him a dish towel to dry his hands.

He did so, then hung it on the rack to dry. Before she knew what he intended, he was standing in front of her, his hands resting on the counter at either side. "Gotcha," he murmured.

"Jon, don't," she warned. "Randall—"

"Is too polite a guest to barge in where he isn't wanted," he finished for her. "I've been wanting to do this all night."

He lowered his head. She fought a brief battle with her conscience, then decided to let him take the kiss. The sooner it was over, the sooner they could return to the other room.

His lips barely grazed hers before withdrawing. She followed his lips instinctively, trying to deepen the kiss, then realized what she was doing.

She placed her hands against his chest. He leaned his weight lightly on them, trapping her hands between them. His mouth grazed hers again . . . a brushstroke that caused the blood to pound in her temples. She sighed shakily.

He nibbled at her lips, little teasing skirmishes that fed the hunger but didn't satisfy it.

"Jon," she murmured, a protest.

"Easy," he whispered against her mouth. "Open to me. I want to taste you."

Helpless, she opened her lips, accepting his tongue, playing the game of advance and retreat with him. It was exciting, and all her nerves were suddenly tingling. She pushed him away and freed her hands, then used them to capture his face and hold it still for the kiss she wanted.

He chuckled deep in his throat and slipped both arms around her, arching her against him. Slowly he rubbed her body with his until the passion roared through her.

She forgot she had a guest waiting only two rooms away. She forgot time and her vow of propriety. In his arms, she found a bliss so potent, she couldn't resist its powerful call. When he released her mouth, she dropped her head back and felt his kisses along her throat. Dizziness washed over her.

"Anne."

She ignored her name and clung to him.

"Anne," Jon said again, low and throaty. "We have to stop. Now. We have to stop now or..."

Opening her eyes—it was an effort—she stared at him, her breath coming in soft gasps from her parted lips.

"We have a guest," he said. "We have to go back."

Reality set in. "Oh," she said, a hand going to her mouth as if to cover the evidence of her wanton conduct.

"Yeah." His eyes crinkled at the corners as he laughed at their predicament. He sucked in a deep breath and let it go in a loud sigh. "Let's get out of here." Taking her hand, he guided her down the hall and into the living room.

"I was wondering if I should send out a search party," Randall said.

"I insisted on helping with the dishes," Jon explained easily. "My mother taught me that was the way to a woman's heart." His eyes flashed over Anne, making her feel warm and strangely cherished.

She brushed her hair back from her temples and smoothed it with fingers that had a tendency to tremble. Randall watched them both without saying anything.

"I have to go. Dawn comes early on the ranch," Jon said.

Hesitantly, she walked him to the door and bid him good-night. He lifted her face with a finger under her chin.

"Don't," she whispered.

"I have to," he replied. He wasn't smiling.

He caught her by her upper arms and bent to her mouth, giving her a kiss on the lips. It was brief, and yet intense.

Anne held herself absolutely still, knowing that Randall could clearly see them from the open arch between the living room and the foyer. She wrapped her arms over her stomach when the kiss ended. "Good night," she said.

He smiled solemnly. "Fourteen to go." He left.

She closed the door abruptly and returned to the living room, taking her customary place on the sofa. Randall moved over beside her. "Alone at last."

Alarm pelted through her. As much as she'd wanted Jon to go, now she wished he'd stayed. Her emotions were in too much of a turmoil for her to be alone with anyone at the present, she realized.

"Did you meet him recently?" Randall asked.

"Saturday." Was that only six days ago? It seemed she'd known him forever. "He came to the bazaar. I'd seen him around town for a week or so before that."

"Hmm." Randall gazed into her eyes. "Has he found the way to your heart?"

His smile was very gentle as he caressed her with the tips of his fingers along her cheek. Tears misted her eyes.

She laughed, but it sounded fake to her ears. "No, of course not."

"But there's something between you. Only a fool could fail to see it."

She was embarrassed at being so transparent. "It isn't anything." At his mild look of reprimand, she added, "Anything important. It isn't anything important."

"You can fool me, but don't fool yourself." He sighed and moved away from her. "If this is the great love of your life, don't let it slip away," he advised solemnly.

She was astounded. "The great love of my life? Don't be ridiculous. It's just... just..." She couldn't think of a word.

"Sex? That's how it usually starts." He reached out and touched her lips. "You've never trembled when I've kissed you."

"Well, of course not. You're a gentleman."

He surprised her by laughing, albeit wryly. "I never realized how insulting that term could be."

"You don't take advantage," she rushed to assure him. Randall never pushed in and demanded more response than she wanted to give.

"Perhaps I should have," he remarked. "But I think it's too late now. He has the upper hand."

She gave him a perplexed glance. "Why do you say that?"

"I've waited for you to accept me. He moved right in and obviously wouldn't take no for an answer. Sometimes that's the best way. Gets right to the heart of the matter."

"Randall—"

"I know. I'm a sweet guy, but I don't turn you on. Jon Sinclair does. When things cool down, I'll be around."

"I'm not hearing this," she muttered.

"Yes, you are." He stood and drew her up to her feet, catching her hands in his. "I wish you felt that way about me." He looked wistful.

"What way?" she demanded. "I'm not in love with the man. It's just a . . . a passion thing."

"Ah, the passion thing," he teased ruefully. He bent forward and kissed her lightly on the lips.

She waited for heart flutters—she *wanted* them—but nothing stupendous happened. Why didn't this really wonderful man make her weak with desire? Why a maverick like Jon Sinclair?

A sigh escaped her.

Randall chucked her under the chin much like her uncle Joe used to do when she was six and despondent about missing her father. "Buck up. Life is easier when you go with the flow."

"Ellen thinks I should have an affair." She bit her lip but the words were out before she could stop them.

He nodded solemnly. "That's probably the only way you'll get it out of your system."

"Like measles?" she asked, exasperated by her friends' attitudes. "Have it and then I'll be immune?"

"Or you'll have it for life," he suggested. He walked to the door, holding her hand as Jon had done.

"He's not a marrying man."

Randall shrugged her statement aside. "Men think that . . . until they're caught." The smile lines deepened at the sides of his mouth. "Stay with it. Decide what you want. Then tell him. What could be easier?"

She frowned, not sure of this advice. "I'll think about it."

Randall kissed her, a soft kiss on the lips that asked for nothing from her. "I've got to get to Beaumont. Sean and I are going fishing at first light."

"Have fun." She patted his arm as he stepped out on the porch. The night air was nippy, and she wrapped her arms across her waist, watching as Randall headed for his car, which was still parked in front of the restaurant.

Across the street, a motor cranked, then hummed quietly. A pickup pulled away from the curb and drove off into the night. She wondered if the driver was Jon and if so, why he'd stay until Randall left. Could it be that he was a little bit worried about the distinguished senator as a rival?

4

Jon hung up the telephone and surged to his feet. He'd successfully renegotiated the livestock contract with the trucking company that would haul this year's cattle to market up in the northern part of the state. Satisfied with the deal, yet oddly restless, he returned to the greenhouse where Pedro was loading mums, already in bloom, onto a truck.

Lifting a wooden crate, Jon flinched with pain. Setting the crate on the truck, he checked his thumb. A long splinter was lodged in the fleshy part, going almost all the way through.

Pedro glanced at it in sympathy. "Better get the splinter out, then clean it good. Maybe you'd better go to the doctor. You had a tetanus shot lately?"

"It'll be all right," Jon muttered, digging his knife out of his pocket. He used the blade to loosen the skin at the edge of the wound and carefully extracted the thin spike of wood from his left thumb. He sucked at the hole and examined it again. Yeah, it looked okay.

He set about getting the flowers loaded. They were supposed to have met the Richport Beautification Committee at the town square ten minutes ago. Pedro's son had called in sick that morning. A hangover, Jon suspected. Pedro looked rather grim. Well, the kid was young. He'd learn not to waste himself on useless binges.

A sense of time speeding by settled on Jon as he and Pedro climbed into the truck and headed for town. He arrived at eight-thirty, only thirty minutes late. The committee was waiting for them. Anne gave him an impatient frown. Ellen Adamson grinned.

"Hi," she called to him. She came over to the truck.

"Thanks for your help with the swooning damsel last week." He nodded toward Anne, who gave him another frown.

"You're late," she told him when he brought the first crate of mums to the flower bed where she was standing.

"Yeah. We were shorthanded."

"What happened to Steve?"

"He called in sick." Jon noted the way the morning sun gave a golden peachy glow to her skin.

She turned to Pedro. "Out again with those guys from the wharves?"

"Yes," Pedro agreed. He looked unhappy.

"We need to find him a nice girl," Anne decided.

From the thoughtful gleam in her eyes, she had someone in mind, Jon decided. "Are you two the committee we were supposed to meet?"

"Yes. We have to get the town square planted today so it will look nice for the judges. They'll be here right before Christmas." She dropped to her knees, pulled on a pair of gloves, picked up a trowel and started setting the mums in the prepared flower bed.

"Judges?" Jon asked, bringing another crate over.

Ellen started at the opposite corner. "Yes, our city is entered in the state community beautification contest. We're determined to win this year. We've been second three years in a row, so it's our turn." She laughed good-naturedly.

Jon found himself smiling, too. Anne's smile was miserly. "Don't crack your face," he taunted softly, setting the flowers down next to her.

"I won't."

He hoisted another load down. "Get up on the wrong side of the bed this morning?" He placed the crate beside her. "Or did the senator keep you up too late last night?"

She gave him a disdainful glance. "He left quite soon after you did. Didn't you see him go?"

Jon shook his head. He'd never admit he'd watched from his truck until the other man left Anne's house. He frowned at the woman who had put him in this jealous state.

She had her hair tucked up under a wide-brimmed hat. In ragged jeans and a long-sleeved shirt, she was adorable.

He paused in surprise. He'd never considered a woman "adorable" before. Neither had he had such a strong desire to touch one. It was unnerving.

Shaking his head slightly, he wondered at the impulse. It wasn't even lustful. He simply wanted to run his fingers along her cheek, to see if she was real. An odd notion.

He grimaced when he set the next crate down too hard and jarred the bruised flesh of his thumb.

"What is this?" Anne demanded.

He peered at the crate, trying to figure out what she saw that bothered her. Probably a bug or worm.

"Blood," she said, bringing her finger up and staring at it. "Where did it come from?" She looked at her hands.

"My thumb," he said, realizing it was oozing bright red drops, which had gotten on some of the flowerpots.

She grabbed his hand and examined his thumb. Her expression became tender and concerned. Hmm, maybe the splinter hadn't been such bad luck after all.

"You've got a splinter in it," she exclaimed.

"Nah. I got it out before we left the ranch."

Ellen came over. "Doc is in his office. You'd better go on over and get it taken care of."

"It's nothing—"

Anne leapt to her feet, still holding his hand. "That's a good idea. He'll probably need a tetanus shot. Come on."

Jon smiled over his shoulder at Ellen, who gave him a wink and a grin, then followed docilely alongside Anne. She pressed a tissue to his wound and murmured soothing things to him.

"Yoo-hoo, Doc? Are you in?" she called, opening the door and barging right into the clinic.

"Back here, Anne."

She led Jon along a corridor and into the doctor's office. "Jon has a splinter in his thumb," she said.

"I got it out," he told the doctor.

"Let me see."

Anne stood aside while Doc checked his thumb. Jon dropped an arm over her shoulder as if he needed support. She looped an arm around his waist. He liked that.

"Ouch," he exclaimed when the doctor pressed his thumb.

"You were right," Doc said to Anne. "There's still something in the wound. Let's go into the examining room."

Jon enjoyed his invalid role as Anne helped him into the next room and urged him to sit on the examining table. He hated to release her, but he hopped up on the table obediently.

"That looks pretty deep. We'd better deaden it." Doc walked toward a cabinet.

"That's okay," Jon told him. "I'll be fine. Go ahead."

Doc frowned, then shrugged. He got out a tray of tools and placed them on a rolling table, which he positioned next to the examining table. "Okay, let's clean this up."

Jon inhaled the warm fragrance of Anne's hair when she pushed her hat off and let it fall against her back, the cord around her neck keeping the hat from dropping to the floor. Her hair was caught in a clip on top of her head. She looked cute as a cowgirl.

"Good enough to eat," he murmured in her ear while the doctor cleaned his thumb. He grinned when she frowned at him, then bent forward to see what was happening to his thumb.

"Shh," she said.

"Hell's bells," Jon said in surprise as pain shot up his arm. He peered at the wound.

The doc was digging around in the puncture hole with something that looked like an X-Acto knife with a long sharp point. Fresh blood welled out of the hole. The doctor swabbed it away with a piece of gauze, then went back to digging in his thumb with the enthusiasm of a woodpecker searching for grubs in a hollow tree.

The room wavered for a second as the pain shot up his arm again. He bit back an expletive, one of the more colorful ones he'd learned in his travels. It was too raunchy for Anne's ears.

Blinking rapidly, he gritted his teeth savagely and held on.

"Lean on me," Anne said softly.

He felt her lift his right arm and put it around her shoulders. For some strange reason, it didn't appear to be attached to the rest of his body. He held on to her as he floated right away.

"Cripes," he ground out when the pain filled his vision with a red haze.

"Yeah, there's a piece of splinter left in there," the doc said. "It's embedded right next to the bone. I'll have to cut it out. Better lie down, Sinclair. This is going to hurt."

"It already does," Jon tried to tell him. The words came out garbled, and he wasn't sure what he said.

"Can you give him a shot?" he heard Anne ask.

The doctor chuckled. "I suspect we'd better. Let's lay him down before he falls."

Jon tried to sit up straight. Slowly his vision cleared as the pain stopped. He realized he was lying down. He saw Anne's face looming over him. She looked like a black-haired angel. "Don't let him amputate." He tried to grin.

"Shh," she said.

"Yes, ma'am," he replied. A new pain attacked his thumb. He turned his head to the side and watched as the doc shot painkiller into the fleshy pad. Soon a cool numbness spread through his hand. "Ahh, better," he said.

"You should have let Doc give you the shot in the first place," she scolded. "Men," she added in disgust.

"Now, now," Doc soothed. He went back to work.

Jon watched Anne's face while the doctor removed the rest of the splinter. He was vaguely aware of stitches being sewn into his thumb, then a bandage being put on and finally, a plastic device being put over it and taped into place.

"How long since you had a tetanus shot?"

He looked at the doctor. "I don't remember ever having one."

"Well, we'd better do it just in case." The doc left the room after pushing the tray of torture instruments aside.

Jon caught Anne's hand, which was smoothing his hair back from his forehead. "Give me a kiss to make it all better?"

She hesitated, then leaned forward. He released her and slipped his hand around her neck. He urged her to his mouth and took the kiss. Her lips moved, then opened provocatively. He felt her tongue stroke his lips. Heat exploded deep inside him.

"Better?" she asked, her voice husky but amused.

"Lots." He felt fine now. The pain was gone, and his head had cleared. He wished they were at her house or his.

She straightened when the doctor returned. Jon sat up gingerly. Yeah, he was all right. Nothing like nearly passing out in front of the woman he wanted to impress. He grinned wryly, recalling her concern and the kiss, which had been more sympathetic than passionate.

"A quick recovery," Doc remarked, grinning. He rubbed Jon's arm with an alcohol pad, then gave him the tetanus shot. "Anne, go get a cup of water from the cooler in the waiting room for our patient. I have a couple of pills for him to take."

Jon watched her bustle out, her hips and legs slender and delectable in her old jeans.

"She's a lovely woman," Doc said, meeting his eyes when Anne had disappeared. "I've known her since she was five. That's when I opened my practice here, straight out of medical school. She's Ellen's best friend."

"You going to ask what my intentions are?"

Doc grinned. "I suspect her aunt already has. Marge has a way of scaring off men who are interested in her niece."

Jon grunted, neither admitting nor denying his interest. "Are you going to warn me off, too?"

"No. I think you might be good for Anne. She's led too sheltered a life. An adventure might be the very thing for her." He smiled with affection. "Be gentle with her."

"I will," Jon heard himself promise.

"Good. Now, one other thing," the doc started matter-of-factly. "I suppose a young, active fellow like yourself has taken the proper precautions?"

Jon felt heat creep up his neck. Was the man talking about what he thought he was talking about? "Precautions?"

"Right," came the blunt reply. "You've been out in the world. Anne hasn't. She might not think ahead. A woman from a small town and all, well, you know how it is. Marge probably turned three shades of purple trying to tell Anne about the birds and bees. She would never be able to handle safe sex."

Jon thought he was going to choke. He couldn't be having this conversation while the woman he wanted with every fiber in him was humming as she returned down the hall.

The doc eyed him balefully. "I've been Anne's doctor since she was a kid. She never takes anything stronger than a vitamin or a headache tablet, you know."

"Uh, no, I didn't," Jon confessed. His ears felt hot. Life in a small town was just as he recalled—nothing was private. He suspected the doc was telling him Anne wasn't on the Pill. He'd already surmised that fact. "Is everyone discussing the kiss at the bazaar?" He'd been pretty stupid to get caught up in passion in front of the whole town.

Doc laughed. "Yeah. We're all watching the battle between you and Anne. The women want her to get you to the altar. The men are rooting for you."

"Oh, great." Just what he wanted, him and Anne the subject of Saturday-night supper at every household in town.

When Anne came in, the doctor dropped a couple of pills in his hand and told him to take them. She handed him the paper cup and looked him over, concern in her eyes, but an encouraging smile on her lips.

"Be sure and change the bandage every day," Doc Adamson advised. "Try not to get it wet. Use some antibiotic cream, too. Here, I'll write the name down for you." He scribbled something on a prescription pad and tore the page off.

Jon stuck the note in his shirt pocket and stood. "I'll pay you now—"

Doc waved the suggestion aside. "Ellen sent you over, so it's free this time. Next time I'll charge double."

Anne took his arm when they went out. He was trying to decide whether to swoon when he saw her gaze on the flowers that still needed to be planted.

He gave up on the idea of her taking him to her house and having him lie down. There were all sorts of things that could lead to, but not today, he decided with a sigh of regret.

"We'd better get back to work," he suggested.

"Your thumb—"

"Will be fine. I can't possibly hurt it now. Pedro is too old to do all the work alone."

"I'll call his son and see if he can help," she decided with a narrowing of her eyes.

Jon grinned. Steve was going to get a lecture on his behavior. He went back to work after assuring Ellen and Pedro that he was going to live.

"Although he looked pretty green there for a while," Anne added cheerfully.

He gave her a severe frown. "You don't have to tell everything," he complained.

She laughed as she headed for her shop to telephone Pedro's son. The sound stayed with him the rest of the morning.

Steve joined them at ten, and shortly after that, a young woman arrived to help. Anne assigned her and Steve to plant the flower bed by the veterans' memorial. By one, all the mums were arranged in attractive designs around the courthouse.

"And it didn't cost the city a cent," Anne said in satisfaction. "All the plants were bought with funds raised by the school kids."

"Is that right?" Jon looked at the bill, which had been paid in full. His father had given a small discount. "I'll match it with an equal amount of plants. You can pick them out, and we'll plant them wherever you want."

"Oh my gosh," she exclaimed. Her smile glowed. She stood on tiptoe and gave him a kiss on the mouth, quick but warm.

"Hmm, Pedro, is there anything else we can give 'em?" he called out, enjoying the color in her face as he teased her.

The others laughed. He glanced at the clock on the bank sign. "How about lunch? My treat."

"I've got to get back to the shop. My aunt is watching it for me, but she has an appointment this afternoon. Thanks for your help, all of you." She dashed off.

Jon frowned as he watched her go. He'd call, he decided, and invite her to dinner. Tonight. Then his place for a nightcap. The townsfolk could wonder what they were doing out there all by themselves!

Ellen sighed and stretched. "I've got to get to the office, too. Doc is probably pulling his hair out...what he has left."

The girl, Lina, also declined with a shy smile. Jon noted Steve's interest when she rushed off.

"She has a father and two brothers to cook for," Steve said.

Jon climbed into the truck. "Let's stop by the pub and pick up some barbecue."

Jon smoothed his tie into place and stepped back from the mirror. He slipped into a blue blazer, then grinned. He looked like some kind of college preppy, out to impress a girl's parents before he seduced their daughter.

A sense of danger invaded the room. He glanced at the bed on his way out. Fresh sheets, clean towels in a freshly scrubbed bathroom—all was ready.

Not that he had any hope of persuading Anne to come home with him. But, hey, a guy could dream.

A warning bell rang through him when he stepped out on the porch and paused, his gaze drawn to the sunset. He was too eager, he admonished. He'd learned long ago not to depend on others. He trusted only himself. But at odd moments that week, he'd had visions of Anne there on the ranch with him, of them working, making love, laughing...

He shook his head. A romantic fool, that's what he was. But the vision wouldn't quite go away.

In town, he noticed the light on and the door open at the Flower Garden. He pulled into a parking space and went into the tiny shop that smelled of fresh juniper.

Ropes of the greenery lined the front windows. Tiny lights winked off and on among the fragrant needles. The place was crammed with Christmas wreaths and potted plants, sachets for gifts, baskets of books, wine and nestled pinecones tied with red bows. Like Anne, the store was a delight to the senses.

"Hi," Anne called out, sticking her head around the edge of the back room doorframe. "I'm almost ready."

He checked his watch. "Take your time. I need a couple of things at the drugstore. I'll run over there."

"Right."

He walked down the street and went into the surprisingly modern drugstore. He had to walk down well-stocked aisles of household and personal goods to get to the drug department. He searched along the shelves until he found the antibiotic ointment and a box of bandages. He couldn't find the other item he wanted.

At the drug counter, he waited patiently for the druggist to finish a phone call, then come from the back and wait on him.

Jon did a double take on the man when he appeared.

"Twins," the druggist remarked. "I'm Dave Adamson. Doc said he worked on your thumb this morning. Ah, I see you got the right stuff."

"Yeah, but there was something else I wanted. Doc said I wasn't to get the bandage wet, but I did when I took a shower. Do you have any finger cots?" He held up his left hand to display the injured thumb.

"Hmm, don't have any calls for those." Dave got a bright-idea look on his face, then rummaged around under the counter. "But I have some samples around here somewhere that might work."

He pulled out a box and read the instructions in fine print on the side. He started to take one packet out, hesitated, looked Jon over, then laid the box on the counter. "Here, try these. They might do the trick."

Jon wasn't sure they had the same use in mind for the product. Could everyone in town see how he felt about Anne?

He pulled out his wallet and got out a twenty-dollar bill to cover the cost of the articles. He noticed Dave tossed the box in the bag but didn't ring up a price when he finished with the other items.

"You...uh...forgot these," he pointed out.

"They're samples. You can have them." Dave grinned. "The salesman said they were a new kind with a, quote, 'soft stretch for a smooth fit,' unquote. He called 'em snuggies."

The heat hit Jon's ears. It had been a few years since he'd blushed like a school kid.

"Uh, thanks," he managed. He took his change, grabbed the bag and hurried out. First a lecture on safe sex and protection. Now, free samples. The twin brothers seemed to be encouraging him to have an affair with Anne. It was damned unnerving.

It occurred to him that neither Dave nor Doc had cautioned him to leave Anne alone. In fact, their only concern seemed to be that she have a good time and was protected from any aftereffects of their passion.

He was still pondering this startling insight when he walked into the flower shop. Anne's aunt stood behind the counter. She gave him a dirty look when he came up to her.

"'Evening, Marge," he said with fake heartiness, and watched her face sour at the familiarity. "How's it going with you?"

"Fine." She regarded him with a suspicious eye. "Anne says you're going out to dinner."

"Yes." He leaned an elbow on the counter and tried to fight the devil that wanted him to say something outrageous to goad the old biddy.

"Anne had a last-minute order to get out." She glared at him as if he had kept the younger woman from her work.

"No rush." He checked his watch and wondered if he should call and change the reservation.

A door slammed in the back. Anne appeared in the doorway. "Hi," she said to him, then spoke to her aunt. "I put the vase in the fridge. The man wants it delivered at nine on the dot. Are you sure it isn't too much trouble? I can call Lina—"

"I don't mind," Marge insisted.

"Thanks, Aunt Marge." She glanced at them as if aware of the tension. "How's your thumb?" she asked Jon.

He glanced at the injured digit. "Okay. There's something I wanted you to do for me. I got the bandage wet in the shower. I wondered if you'd mind changing it?" He tossed the bag of first-aid supplies on the counter.

"Not at all." Anne took the package and shook out the contents. A tube of first-aid ointment dropped out, then a flip-top tin of various-size bandages and last...

He muttered an expletive and grabbed at the box of condoms when they landed with a, to him, deafening clatter on the glass countertop near Anne's pickle-faced aunt. He'd completely forgotten about those.

In his haste to hide them before the women realized what they were, he banged his sore thumb, which dislodged his grip on the incriminating evidence.

The damned box leapt gleefully into the air, then teetered on his fingertips, pirouetting as gracefully as a ballerina so that they all got a good look at it before it spun gracefully from his desperate attempts to hold on, slid across the countertop, lingered teasingly at the edge, then tumbled to the floor, landing with a plump *smack* at the feet of the Wicked Witch of the West, otherwise known as Aunt Marge.

She bent and lifted the box. Tilting her head back so she could train her bifocals on the fine print, she held the box high and read the pink lettering. "'Snuggies,'" she read aloud, a perplexed expression on her face. "'A soft stretch for a smooth fit.'"

Jon groaned silently. He knew the exact moment the aunt realized their use.

She gasped, dropped the box as if it contained a lethal poison that could kill by proximity and laid a hand to her heart as two spots of red flamed in her face.

Anne picked it up, read the name, then tucked the package back into the sack. The imp of mischief laughed at him from her blue-violet eyes. Then she started laughing aloud.

Jon felt the blood pound in his ears. The aunt's face was an interesting shade of scarlet. He thought his probably matched it. Anne, who had no sense of dignity at all, as he was rapidly discovering, tried to hide her laughter in a cough, started to choke, then nearly strangled.

He decided if she lived, *he* was going to choke her.

"Free samples. Dave. At the drugstore. Didn't have finger cots," he muttered, realizing how incoherent his explanation sounded and wishing he was anyplace but here.

He wondered when he'd gone from wanting to taunt the aunt to wanting to impress her. Then he wondered what the hell his change of heart meant. It was damned confusing.

Anne managed to contain her uncalled-for merriment.

Jon wasn't sure Marge was breathing, she stood so still. However, the red tide of embarrassment was leaving her face, and the sour-pickle look was returning.

He breathed a sigh of relief. He'd been afraid he might have to do CPR on her, a thought to make grown men quake. He asked, with a show of proper concern, if she was all right.

She glared at him and snorted indignantly. He wouldn't have been surprised if she'd called the cops and had him arrested for insulting her sensibilities.

Anne, the irreverent one, clamped both hands over her mouth, but laughter bubbled out anyway. Jon felt the heat light up his face once more. By damn, he *was* going to choke her!

"Do we look that desperate?" she asked brazenly.

"Well, I am, but I wasn't sure about you," he admitted, taking his cue from her on how to handle the situation.

"Anne, I don't think you should encourage this kind of talk," Marge said, her glare hot enough to produce cinders.

Naturally it was directed at him and not her snickering niece. He gave Anne a look meant to be stern, then lost it as he took in her outfit and the delectable curves and soft shadows they caused in the smooth-fitting material. She was beautiful.

Anne noted his gaze taking in her black knit slacks and the matching top. She had chosen to wear gold chain earrings and a gold necklace with the outfit. She hoped she looked casual but chic. He'd mentioned a place on the river that tried to look like a fisherman's hangout, but no one was fooled. It was posh and expensive.

"I suppose we should mind our manners," she told Jon, smiling into his eyes as if they shared a wonderful secret and weren't telling what it was.

She removed the thumb guard and the wet bandage. After drying his thumb with a tissue, she dabbed on fresh ointment, wrapped a new bandage around it and replaced the guard.

"There, all fixed."

Beside her, she felt her aunt's anger, but it was a distant thing, not impinging upon her sense of happiness at all.

"Ready?" he asked.

She nodded, aware of the husky depth of his voice. "I'll see you tomorrow, Aunt Marge."

"Don't stay out late," Marge advised tersely.

Jon opened the door. "Don't wait up," he called over his shoulder. Then, in a low tone as they walked to his truck, he added, "We might not come in at all. I have a hankering to see the dawn with you."

"I'm glad you didn't say that in front of Aunt Marge. She already thinks you're an evil influence."

"I certainly hope so," he admitted, opening the truck door for her.

"Me, too. By the way, you blush the most becoming shade of red—sort of fire engine with undertones of brick—"

"Don't push your luck," he warned. "Your laughter didn't help the situation at all."

"I know." She tried to sound contrite.

He gave her a withering glance. After he was in, but before he drove off, he tossed the bag into the glove compartment. Anne thought of the contents. She started laughing again.

"It wasn't that funny." He drove down the street.

"I thought Aunt Marge was going to faint . . . or hit you with something. I wouldn't have missed that for a million dollars."

"Actually, I'd forgotten about those. When you appeared, I forgot about everything. You look gorgeous."

"Thank you. I did it all for you."

Their eyes met when he stopped for a red light. She gave him a deliberately sexy look. The temperature went up several degrees in the truck.

"How long do we have to do the mating ritual?" he asked.

"Until after dinner?" she suggested.

"I should have chosen a place closer to town," he muttered. The light changed and he took off.

They arrived at the restaurant a few minutes late and were taken to their table.

"Ah, a view of the river—how nice." She took the chair Jon held for her. His fingers touched lightly on her shoulders before he sat in the chair on the side adjacent to her rather than opposite. It was more intimate.

"You smell good," he told her after the hostess left.

"So do you." She smiled into his eyes, feeling the excitement building like a summer afternoon thunderstorm as layer upon layer of tempestuous energy formed between them.

They ate grilled fish with toasted almonds. Everything tasted wonderful to her. Jon ordered wine with the meal. They finished off the bottle.

"Biscotti and coffee?" he asked later.

She nodded. His mood was thoughtful. She'd witnessed flashes of passionate interest in his eyes, but then it would be gone, replaced by emotions she couldn't read.

"Do you want to dance?" he eventually asked. He dipped one end of a biscotti slice into his coffee and held it out to her.

She ate the cookie before it crumbled. She fed him from her piece. It seemed very romantic, not at all like the political dinners she'd been to recently where she'd felt she must always guard her thoughts. One fling...

When he enfolded her into his arms on the crowded dance floor, she sighed and closed her eyes. This felt right.

His cheek touched her temple. He guided both her arms around his neck and placed both his arms around her waist, drawing her closer. She was aware of all the places they touched along their bodies...and the desire he couldn't conceal when they were this close.

"Why does the doc and his cousin and his twin brother want us to have an affair?" Jon murmured close to her ear.

"I didn't know they did."

"Ellen directed me to your house last Saturday. Today she ordered me to the doctor, who happens to be her employer and cousin. The doc and the druggist seemed very hopeful about an involvement between us. It makes a man suspicious."

"Think you're about to get trapped into marriage like that neighbor girl tried to do when you were eighteen?"

"How did you know about that?"

"Doc told me." She leaned her head back and felt the sweep of her hair against her knit top. She realized she felt vitally alive and very sexy. "You don't have to worry. I'm not going to demand marriage, no matter what happens between us."

He lifted his head to study her. "Yeah? What makes you different from other women?"

"I know what I want. If I marry, it won't be you." She studied his handsome, albeit disbelieving, expression. "Poor darling. Have very many women tried to lure you to the altar?" She gazed at him in teasing sympathy.

"A couple."

"I've had the same problem with men."

"So why didn't you accept one of them?"

"I like my independence," she explained. "Plus I have money. My father puts about half of what he makes in a mutual fund for me. I've rarely used any of it since I make a living with the shop. So you see, I have nothing to gain from marriage but a man to clutter up my life.''

''Hmm,'' he said. ''What about the senator?''

''We're just good friends.'' She batted her eyelashes at him and wondered if she was letting the wine go to her head.

''Now why do I doubt that?''

She laughed and snuggled close. ''Let's not quarrel.''

''Right.''

But she was aware of his doubts. He wasn't quite sure what an involvement with her would mean. But he would learn.

With her, he was entirely safe from entanglements of a permanent nature. She wouldn't marry him even if he begged. It wouldn't be right, and she always tried to play fair.

5

Jon pulled into the drive at his house, but he didn't stop by the steps. Instead, he drove along the gravel road beside the greenhouses and the rows of flowering perennials until he reached a swamp willow on the bank over the creek. He turned off the engine and rolled down his window.

Anne rolled the window on her side down, too. The cool night breeze sighed through the cab of the truck.

"Beautiful," she murmured, her smile visible in the soft glow of moonlight that limned the trees and shrubs along the bank and set pools of molten pewter running through the troughs of the wavelets on the river.

He smiled, too, but for a different reason. "I feel like a sixteen-year-old," he told her, "bringing my date to the river to park, hoping I get a chance to do more than kiss her."

"Are you going to grope me?"

He heard the amusement in her tone and wondered why she didn't take their attraction seriously. "Nothing so crude."

Moving closer on the bench seat, he slipped an arm around her shoulders and turned sideways. She sighed and leaned her head into the crook of his elbow.

"Nice," she whispered.

He feathered kisses along her temple and down her cheek. "Very nice," he agreed. He explored the dimples at the corners of her mouth before paying proper respect to her lips. Brushing his mouth across hers, he felt the tremor that raced through her as she turned more fully to him and caressed his shoulders.

He gave a low growl and took her mouth in a deep, sensuous kiss that quickly skyrocketed out of control. When her hands touched his bare skin, he, too, trembled with unexpected need.

Breathing harshly, he broke the kiss and pressed her head to his chest to stop the exchange.

"Don't stop," she implored, kissing him through his shirt while her hands continued caressing his back.

With a sharp intake of breath, he realized she'd pulled his shirt loose so she could run her hands under it. The feel of her hands on his flesh was the sweetest torment he'd ever known.

"I've never been so hot for a woman. If I weren't a gentleman, I'd take you right here."

She lifted her head. "Why don't you?"

"Don't say things like that." His laughter was a trifle shaky. "I'm already at the boiling point."

Her hands slipped forward on him until she could stroke her fingers across his nipples. She proceeded to drive him wild with her caresses.

"If I do that to you, will it make you crazy?" he mused.

"Definitely."

She stretched up and nipped at his lips, then sucked the bottom one into her mouth and ran her tongue over it until he was close to exploding. Only a firm reminder of the pit he could be digging for himself held him back.

However, he wasn't over the edge yet.

Finding the hem of her sexy knitted top, he slipped a hand under it until he could touch the satin expanse of skin. She arched instinctively against him.

"You're the most naturally passionate woman I've ever met," he told her when she released him.

"Because of you," she said breathlessly.

He held her a few inches away and studied her expression. Warnings chimed inside him, so far from the reality of holding her that he barely heard them. He heaved a deep sigh, then slid his hands upward until he cradled her breasts in his palms.

Like the first kiss under the Christmas Kisses—$1.00 sign, he marveled at how womanly she felt to him . . . as if she were the archetype of all females who had gone before and would come afterward in this crazy, mixed-up world.

When her nipples beaded, he pressed his forehead to hers. "Your response makes me want to see what you would do if I kissed you there." He circled her nipples with the tips of his fingers, feeling the sensitivity to his touch. "And then I wonder what else would happen. . . ."

"I'd come apart."

"Yes. *Yes.*"

Anne smiled at the passion in him. When he pressed, she let herself slip back until she half reclined in the corner of the seat. He followed her. With a deft maneuver, he unfastened her bra and pushed it out of the way.

The cool air hit her breasts, followed a second later by the moist caress of his mouth as he moved from one to the other, nibbling and tasting until she burned with needs she hadn't fully realized she had.

Worry flitted through her mind—that she might want more than a brief affair with this man. No, she'd decided long ago not to marry a man who'd want children from her. She wouldn't pass on the curse she'd lived under all her life. All she wanted was an affair—a brief, beautiful fling with no regrets on either side when it was over.

For a second, fear clamped a cold hand on her heart. This man stirred her as no other had ever done. What if she fell head over heels in love?

No, she promised herself, she wouldn't. She'd be careful. She'd watch her emotions. She'd play the game with a light hand and a wary heart. That way, no one would get hurt.

The door handle gouged into her side. She squirmed, and Jon lifted himself off her. "Sorry, I didn't mean to mash you."

She sat up when he did and drew a shaky breath. "Why are we making out in a truck when your house is right down the road? Beds were invented before vehicles for a good reason." She rubbed the spot on her side.

"Because I don't intend to go that far with you."

The news floored her. "You don't?" Her disbelief and disappointment were obvious. She searched for something to say. "I'm not dangerous to your freedom."

He didn't answer.

"Jon?"

"Something doesn't jibe here. Doc, Ellen and Dave seem to have decided we should have an affair. It doesn't make sense."

"Don't be so suspicious," she told him. She straightened her clothes and ran her fingers through her hair. She was more than annoyed by his caution. She was insulted. "I'll put it in writing—I wouldn't marry you if you begged me."

"Yeah? Why not?"

"I prefer older men. Like Randall."

"You're not in love with him, and you don't want him the way you want me. It would never work. You'd think of me and wonder what you'd missed every time you made love.''

"What an ego.'' She covered her mouth over a yawn. "If we're not going to your house, then I'd like to go home. I have a busy day tomorrow. The holidays are hectic, you know.''

He peered at her through the dim light that filtered into the truck. With a sudden move, he laid his fingertips to the pulse in her neck. "You're not as calm as you act.''

She pushed his hand away. "Yes, I am. I'm over my mad rush of passion. Now I'm merely sleepy.''

"I could bring it back.''

"It's too late. The mood is gone.''

"You're angry.''

"The aftereffects of thwarted desire,'' she snapped. She really was angry, and she couldn't figure out why. It was probably wiser not to succumb to the physical yearning he stirred in her, but his wariness stung her pride.

He leaned close to study her in the soft light of the moon. "Something is strange here. People in small towns are supposed to be conservative and morally rigid. Why are they pushing us toward licentious behavior?''

"Beats me.''

He leaned into his corner of the truck with one arm dangling over the steering wheel. Even without light, she could detect suspicion bristling from him like quills on a cornered porcupine.

He ran a hand through his hair. "Should I start shopping for a gift for you and the senator?''

"Not yet. It'll probably be a while before I commit myself for life.'' She adopted a sexy, teasing tone. "After knowing you, I might not want anyone when you're gone, not for a while.''

"Thanks. It's good to know I'll be missed." He sounded disgruntled.

"But while you're here, I'll be faithful. I'll expect the same from you," she told him.

"A temporary, but binding commitment," he mused aloud. "I'll think about it."

"Thanks." She wondered why men thought they could have an affair and leave, but a woman couldn't. "I'd like to go home now. We're going to plant the borders around city hall tomorrow."

"I remember." He started up the truck and backed around onto the road. Driving past his house, he fought an urge to stop and take her inside. Something was weird in this town. He couldn't figure out what it was. He should sell the ranch and get the hell out of there. But he knew he wasn't going to.

Not yet.

Ellen rushed over to Anne as soon as the Sunday morning service was over. "Well?" she demanded.

"Well, what?" Anne squinted against the light that hit her eyes when they stepped outside.

"How was your date last night?"

"Dinner was delicious, the conversation was scintillating and the music was nice."

Ellen made a face. "Is that all—food, talk and music?"

Anne had to laugh at her friend's disappointment. "Yes. And you, Doc and Dave can quit plotting."

"Plotting?"

"Innocence doesn't become a woman of your age."

"Ouch!" Ellen rubbed the imaginary spot where the barb went in. "You're in a terrible mood this morning. Nothing happened, huh? That's a shame."

Anne looked heavenward. "Please don't let me hit my best friend here in front of the whole town," she prayed aloud.

"Anne? Anne!" a voice called behind them.

"Oh, oh, the gorgon approaches."

Anne smothered laughter as her aunt came abreast of them. "Good morning, Aunt Marge."

Marge spoke to both women, then to her niece. "Anne, you are coming to the country club for lunch with us, aren't you?"

"I can't. The beautification volunteers are going to plant the raised beds at city hall."

Her aunt frowned. "On Sunday?"

"It's the only afternoon most of us have free," Anne pointed out patiently.

"You could join us," Ellen suggested brightly, knowing Marge hated gardening.

Marge gave her a disdainful glance, then turned back to Anne. "Don't overdo. You fainted last weekend at the bazaar. Remember your condition."

"I'll be fine," Anne assured the older woman. She kissed her cheek affectionately. Aunt Marge might be irritating, but she'd been the closest thing to a mother that Anne had ever had.

"She drives me up the wall," Ellen said after Marge had hurried off to join her husband.

"I know, but she means well. Did you know she lost two children soon after their births?"

"No. What happened?"

"One lived a day, the other about a week. They both had defective hearts."

"What kind of defects?"

Anne shrugged. "I don't know the details."

As a teenager, she'd tried to question her aunt about it a couple of times. Her aunt had burst into tears. It had been so shocking, seeing stalwart Aunt Marge cry, that Anne hadn't dared ask again. The same thing had happened when Anne had asked about her mother's death.

"Aunt Marge lost her sister and her own two children within a couple of years of each other," Anne concluded, her heart filled with tenderness toward her aunt, who had loved and cared for her as if she were her own.

Ellen stared thoughtfully at the departing car that carried the mayor and the councilwoman. "That's sad."

"Yes. Well, I'm going home to change. I'll meet you at city hall. The deli is bringing free lunches for all the workers, so don't eat anything."

A half hour later, Anne sat on the grass at the city hall building, which was on one corner of the huge courthouse square. The neat brick structure had matching flower boxes along the walk leading to the front door and across the front of the building. She was envisioning it as it would look when the flowers were in.

"Here comes your dream man," Ellen said.

Anne glanced across the lawn and spotted Jon walking toward them. He was dressed in khaki walking shorts and sneakers. His shirt hung open, exposing a tempting expanse of tanned flesh.

Her gaze was irresistibly drawn to the mat of hair on his chest, to the muscles rippling along his torso as he moved, the neat indentation of his belly button . . .

"You're staring," Ellen warned.

"Mmm-hmm."

Her friend cocked her head to one side and studied Jon. When he dropped to the grass in front of them and opened his box lunch, she spoke. "Anne thinks you look good enough to eat."

Anne shot Ellen a threatening glance over the rim of her lemonade cup before taking a long, cool swallow.

Jon looked her over for a long minute before replying. "Tell her she does, too."

"He thinks you look ravishing," she said to Anne, then turned back to Jon. "Are you two not speaking?"

"I'm not sure. You'll have to ask her." He opened the wrapper on the turkey sandwich and bit a chunk out.

"Are you not speaking?" she asked Anne.

"I am. I don't know about him. Hi, Jon," she added.

"Hi, Anne."

The deep, quiet tone of his voice vibrated right down to her toes. She forced herself to look him in the eye.

It was like looking into a silver-coated surface—all reflection and no depths. No silent laughter at their mutual plight. No spark of delight at her presence. And no warm, lusty passion reaching out to her in a visual caress.

She missed it.

"Well," she said, ignoring the stab of regret, "I suppose I'd better organize the work parties. Pedro and Steve have started unloading the plants from the truck."

She stood, brushed crumbs off her work shirt and called the volunteers around her. She assigned planters and handed out sketches showing where the flowers should go. She noticed Steve moving flats within easy reach of Lina and felt a slight catch in the vicinity of her heart. Things were perking along there.

Two days in a row, the young man had shown up at the shop and driven the part-time helper home after work. She'd overheard him tell Lina that he was thinking of signing up for horticultural classes at the local college. Lina was learning flower arranging as well as the business of the shop. Anne hoped to make the younger woman the manager in a few years.

"Plant them a little closer," she advised the woman who'd been her high school English teacher.

When everyone was working to her satisfaction, she knelt beside a planter and began putting the flowering bulbs into the ground. An off-duty policeman worked toward her from the other end of the planter.

A shadow fell across her. Jon placed a tray on the ground beside the flower bed. "Pedro and I are going to get the second load. We should be back in an hour."

"Good. We'll be ready for the next batch by then. Umm, we'll probably be finished in front, so drive around to the back of the building. The police station needs sprucing up, too."

He nodded and left.

She watched him stride away with a sort of hungry ache in the pit of her stomach. It wasn't fair that one man had so much appeal. Just looking at his bare skin made her want to run her hands all over his lean, muscular hide.

Seventy-three minutes later, she groaned and stood. She stretched her tired back, then did a few limbering exercises.

"Me, too," Lina said, coming up behind her.

The young woman was twenty-three and still lived at home, taking care of her father and brothers. Perhaps it was time for both of them to "get a life," as the saying went.

Anne peered down the road. "I wonder where Jon and Pedro are. They were supposed to have returned by now."

"I hope they haven't had an accident."

Anne suppressed her anxiety. "I'm sure they haven't. I hope they get here soon. I'm worried the volunteers will leave before we're finished if we don't keep them working."

"You're right about that," the policeman said, tamping the mound of dirt around the last flower from his tray. "There go the chief's kids, sneaking off through the park."

Sure enough, two boys slipped out of sight behind some trees before anyone else noticed they were gone. The youngsters, sons of the fire chief, were the terror of the town.

Last week, they'd tied Aunt Marge's big tomcat to the English teacher's Doberman with a ten-foot rope, then climbed a tree to watch the action. Unfortunately, the cat had climbed the same tree. The nine- and eleven-year-old brothers had found themselves face-to-face with one mad feline. With the furious dog snarling from the ground, ready to attack whatever dropped into its jaws, they were trapped.

The fire department had rescued the boys from the very top of the sycamore... after coaxing the dog into letting a fireman untie the rope that bound him to the cat and then coaxing the cat to let him lift it from its safety perch. The fire chief had grounded the boys for a year.

"Should we tell the chief his sons are on the loose?"

The policeman smiled. "We'd better. No telling what they'll get into if we don't. I'll take care of it." He strode off toward the firehouse on the next block.

Anne glanced at her watch. Jon and Pedro should have been back by now. The jingle of a bell interrupted her thoughts.

She'd arranged for lemonade to be delivered in midafternoon, thinking they'd be through with their work by now. No such luck.

"Great," Steve said eagerly. "I'll bring yours," he told Lina. He raced a couple of teenage boys and got in line first.

Anne waited until everyone was served, then went to get a drink for herself. Hearing a strange noise up the street, she stopped . . . then stared, mouth agape.

A stampede was coming down the middle of Main Street, heading straight for the courthouse.

"Oh, no," she cried, "not the mums." She raced to head the beasts off before they trampled all the flowers that had been planted the previous day.

She heard running steps behind her. Steve and the two teenagers passed her. They were too late. A hundred cows galloped across the smooth lawn and plowed right over the waving stands of mums, throwing divots of grass and flowering bulbs into the air in their wake.

Anne gazed in disbelief at the destruction. "Those brats!" she yelled over the receding thunder of hooves. "I'm going to hang them by their big toes from the Victory oak!"

The oak had been planted in the courthouse yard at the end of World War II and was now a good-size tree. She stopped by its sturdy trunk and glared while the herd swept down the entire front lawn of the old-fashioned courthouse. So much for the beautification contest.

Walking over to a once-colorful flower bed in the middle of the sweeping lawn, she knelt and lifted one perfect mum on its mangled stalk. When she released it, the flower fell to the ground like a swooning maiden whose legs had buckled.

"I'll tie them up and make them eat spinach for a year," she muttered. "And no television for the rest of their lives."

"Anne, look out," Ellen screamed.

She glanced around and saw Ellen pointing to a spot behind her. Then she started, too surprised to be scared.

A bull stood at the corner of the trampled lawn. His head was down and he pawed the grass, sending up a spray of dirt and grass and flower pieces. He gave a bellow that started out low and rose to a crescendo of anger.

Anne thought maybe she was in trouble.

Jon gunned the engine when the herd of frightened cows were past the truck and he sped toward the courthouse lawn. The front tires of the truck jumped the curb before he could get stopped. He leapt from the cab before the vehicle came to a complete halt and raced toward the oak tree and Anne.

"Behind the tree," he shouted. "Get behind the tree."

Relief washed over him when Anne realized what he was telling her and darted for the oak. The enraged bull charged.

"Haaaaaiiii," he shouted, flapping his arms like mad.

The creature swung its massive head toward this new menace.

"Yeah, over here, big fellow," Jon coaxed, stopping a few feet in front of the bull. He yanked his shirt off.

The adrenaline pumped through him, and he went into a cool, clear-thinking mode, one he'd first experienced when facing a group of tramps intent on robbing him his first night riding the rails when he'd left home.

He shook the shirt at the bull. The bull charged, but without much speed at this close range, and followed the shirt as Jon swept it back like a matador's cape.

Around him, he was aware of someone giving orders and clearing the street of bystanders while he kept the bull engaged. He backed up a few feet when the animal stopped and whirled with an angry bellow. "Hey," he called the way the bullfighters did in movies. "Hey."

The bull charged again. This time it dipped its head and hooked left with its horns. One caught the shirt and jerked it from his hands, the other grazed the skin across his stomach, making a stinging welt in its passage.

"Close call," he muttered. He needed that shirt back.

The bull shook his head until the shirt was dislodged from its horns, then proceeded to grind it into the dirt.

"So much for one good shirt," Jon said. He started to unsnap his khaki shorts but saw he didn't have time. The bull had spotted him again and was heading his way. He bit off an expletive and prepared to dive to the side at the last minute.

From the corner of his eye, he caught movement.

"Hey, over here, bozo," Anne called out. She waved her arms and ran forward until the bull noticed her.

Jon did the same.

It stopped and pawed the ground nervously, not sure whom to attack. When it started toward him again, another voice joined in. The policeman who'd been helping with the planting clapped his hands and called to the creature. Steve and the teenagers joined in, further confusing the animal.

The bull swung in a circle, charging a few steps toward one person, then another, unable to decide who was the enemy.

A man appeared with a rifle. Anne bit her lip to keep from crying out a protest. Human life was at stake here.

The shot rang out. The bull let out a bellow and ran a few steps, then stopped in confusion. Anne saw a hypodermic jutting from the animal's neck and smiled in relief.

The tranquilizer acted fast. First the hind legs buckled, then the front. The vet handed the rifle to one of the teenagers and ran across the lawn. He dodged the horns as the frightened animal tried to hook him and gave it a shot.

In another minute, all was under control.

Anne picked up Jon's shirt. "I think this has seen its better days," she remarked, smiling at him.

He gave her a grim look, grabbed the shirt, shook the grass off and put it on. It had one long tear across the front.

"Let me see your injury," she requested, bending to inspect the welt across his waist. The skin had broken in a couple of places and droplets of blood rose to the surface, fused and slowly ran down into the waistband of his shorts. "Come on. We'll go to my house and treat that."

He glanced at the welt, then stepped back from her when she would have touched him. She straightened. "Was it something I said?" she inquired, meeting his gaze squarely.

A startled expression crossed his face, then he shook his head. "I'm all right."

Ellen joined them. "Well, that was enough excitement to last a lifetime. I thought you were a goner when I saw that beast charge at you." Her concerned gaze searched over Anne, then Jon. "That was very brave of you," she told him.

"Nah. In my wilder days, some friends and I used to go down to the stock pens and pretend we were famous bullfighters. I learned then that the critters followed motion."

"So that's the secret. I thought it was the red cape they didn't like. You know, seeing red and all that. Well, one more illusion down the drain."

Anne had the feeling that Ellen was chatting to ease the strain between her and Jon. She couldn't figure out why there was this distance between them.

A reporter for the local paper came over and another from the local radio station. The next couple of hours were spent in rehashing the events. Things calmed down after that.

The beautification crew examined the ruined grounds. "I guess we won't win a prize," Lina remarked.

Everyone burst into laughter. They lifted mums and convulsed when the poor things collapsed. They threw petals into the air and generally acted like fools until the nervous energy caused by the emergency dissipated.

"Hey, there are mums in the field at the ranch," Jon told them when they assembled to decide what to do. "We can dig them out and replant. If you guys are willing."

"Those are your seed bulbs," Anne protested. "We can't take those. That's next year's mums."

"There'll be enough left. Anyway, when the blooms are gone, I can collect the bulbs."

"Great," someone called out. "Let's get started."

"You'd better come out and pick the colors. I don't have enough yellow and white ones to replace the trampled ones. You'll have to go to another color scheme."

"Let's do an English garden—a mass of colors, all mixed up," she decided. She grinned. "This will be fun."

Over a hundred new volunteers showed up to help and talk about the stampede and the bullfight. She and Jon organized them into work groups, raking up the debris. The mayor sent a truck over to haul the wreckage to the dump.

"Where do you suppose those Ralston kids got to?" one of the teenagers asked.

"We don't know that they did it."

Jon glanced at Anne when she said this. Her friend, Ellen, rolled her eyes. She obviously believed the kids were guilty.

"Ready to go?" he asked Anne. "You can choose which flowers you want and we'll put a crew to digging them up."

He selected Steve, the two teenagers who'd helped hold the bull at bay, Lina and six others to accompany them to the ranch. Anne left Ellen in charge of the cleanup.

"I'll meet you out there," Anne said, heading for her house.

"You can ride in the truck. In front," he added, motioning the rest into the back. Everyone climbed in. He noticed Anne did so reluctantly.

His change in attitude confused her, but it couldn't be helped. He'd realized he couldn't have a flaming affair with her, then skip town. It wasn't that simple, not anymore. Since meeting her, life had become infinitely complex.

The thought came to him that he might not want to leave.

He backed the truck carefully off the sidewalk and headed for the ranch. A sweet tantalizing odor drifted through the cab of the truck. He recognized the faint scent of her perfume.

His body reacted immediately. He wanted to take her to his house and make love to her for hours on end.

Cool it, he advised his raging libido. Passion was one of the natural results of an adrenaline kick after the danger was past. But the rationalization did nothing to ease the throbbing clamor in his loins, he found.

Anne looked out the window and didn't speak the entire trip to the ranch. The atmosphere was nothing like the trip last night. Then, the air had been filled with expectancy. Until he'd come to his senses.

"Anne," he said. Her name came out soft, like a caress. He cleared his throat and aimed for a business tone. "I can't have an affair with you and then sell out and leave as if nothing had happened. It wouldn't be fair to you."

She turned to him. Again she surprised him with the candor and humor in her eyes. "Even if I tell you that's all I want?"

"Women always want to sentence a man for life."

"I've already told you my views on that."

He gave her a skeptical glance. "Huh."

Her laughter floated over him, an adorable sound. There was that word again—*adorable*.

"Thanks for your help with the bull," he remembered to say. "I thought I'd have a heart attack when I saw it charge you."

"That was the most frightened I've ever been." She laid a hand on his arm. "Take care of that scrape when we get to your house. Promise."

He nodded. She confused him. She seemed to care, but she didn't want a future with him. Something didn't add up here.

She settled back to watching the scenery.

When they arrived at the ranch, he opened the glove compartment and removed the sack of first-aid supplies. He recalled the fiasco in front of her aunt. Anne had laughed. He'd miss her sense of humor when he left. She was a good sport about life, not complaining once about the heart condition her aunt had told him about.

She smiled when she saw the sack. After climbing out, she waited for him in front of the truck and chatted with Lina.

Jon smeared the ointment along the scrape, then threw the things back in the compartment. He gazed at the box of snuggies for a second and shook his head slightly, denying the need that wouldn't quite go away.

They walked the fields. "This is beautiful." She waved an arm to indicate the acres of brilliant color from flowering bulbs. "How about if we feature this on our community fund-raising tour? We could charge a dollar extra per person and pay you back—"

"I don't want any money. I'll have the bulbs, so I won't be losing anything."

She studied him for a minute. "You're a good man, Charlie Brown," she teased lightly, then went on.

An hour later, when they were ready with the first load, the fire chief drove up. He and his two kids got out. The boys were subdued and frightened.

"These guys have something to say to you," Chief Ralston told Anne. He gave his boys a stern look.

The oldest one apologized first, then the younger.

"They'll be turning over their savings to you tomorrow," the chief informed them. "To pay for the replanting. And then..." His tone made it plain they were in deep trouble.

"Oh, no," Anne protested. "That's their college fund. They want to be veterinarians," she explained to Jon.

He took one look into her pleading eyes and was sunk. "I could use some help. How about if they work it off? Say, after school and on Saturdays until the end of the year? I'll deduct the cost from their pay."

The two contrite boys stared at Jon. Then the youngest burst into tears and threw his arms around Anne's waist. "We didn't mean to hurt anybody," he sobbed. "We didn't know a bull had been put in with the cows. When I saw him go after you..." He cried harder.

Anne held him and ran her fingers over his hair, soothing the child with crooning noises. "I'm okay," she murmured. "I know you didn't mean any harm."

Jon watched them for a second, then turned away. His breath jammed in his throat and his chest went all tight and achy. Anne would be good with kids.

The thought lingered in his mind like the notes of a melody he couldn't dislodge. He kept seeing her, walking across the flower-laden fields at the ranch, a black-haired, blue-eyed girl holding her hand while a black-haired boy raced ahead.

He found himself trying to envision the boy's face . . . to see if his eyes were dark, like the senator's.

Or gray. Like his.

With a curse, he cleared his mind and concentrated on the task at hand. Marriage and kids weren't in the cards for him. No way. Definitely out. He'd made that clear at the start.

For a second, he wondered who he was trying to convince— himself or her.

6

→←

Anne sighed happily at five that afternoon. Unbelievably, the flower beds were all replanted in a glorious mix of fall colors. Instead of the more formal aspect of the earlier planting, this one was a riot of double and triple blooms.

She'd chosen a rainbow effect, going from white to yellow, orange, red, magenta to almost black, using variegated plants to make the transition from one color to another.

"I like it better," Ellen declared. "The effect is stunning, simply stunning."

A group of kids, led by the teenagers who'd proven their worth that day, had smoothed and replaced the grass divots so that the lawn looked pretty good, too. It would be fine when the judges arrived, Anne thought. She sighed again.

Jon stretched and rotated his shoulders, working out the kinks. Like most of the young men, he'd removed his shirt while working. He stood with his legs planted apart, his hands on his hips as he checked the flower beds, and nodded in approval.

He looked like a warrior, she thought—proud and brave, tested by battle and grown wise with time.

She'd watched him with the young people. He'd directed them in a no-nonsense manner, yet he'd treated them as people with ideas and thoughts of their own that were worth sharing. He'd make a good father.

A stillness developed inside her, and a picture formed in her mind of Jon with a son, teaching him all the things a man needed to know. She forced the image away.

She wasn't going to think of him that way. Whatever kind of father he would someday become was no business of hers.

Turning toward the workers who now sprawled in tired poses on the courthouse steps or in the grass, she thanked them for their help and told them to keep their fingers crossed regarding the beautification contest.

"Thanks for being the hero of the day," she said softly to Jon. She let her eyes feast on him for another second before dragging her gaze away.

"Some hero," he scoffed with becoming modesty.

A surge of affection washed over her. She'd never met a man with so many endearing traits. "You saved my life when the bull charged. I didn't know what to do."

"You repaid that when you distracted him from goring me."

She laughed. "So we're both wonderful."

"Yeah." And he just looked at her.

"See you later." She walked home, aware of the fatigue that throbbed in her arms and legs, the heaviness in her chest.

At the house, she took two aspirin, then soaked in a tub of the hottest water she could stand.

Thirty minutes later, she slipped on a long cotton-knit nightgown and went into the kitchen. She wondered what Jon was having for supper. After eating a simple dish of pasta and fresh vegetables, she watched the news on TV and skimmed through a magazine. The house seemed lonely.

Her father had given the place to her when he'd had to make his headquarters in New York a few years ago. He was coming home for Christmas this year, but she wasn't sure what day he would arrive. He called and sent whimsical little gifts often, but she was lonely for him, for his comforting presence.

She needed to ask him things, man-woman things, so maybe she could understand life better. She wanted to ask about her mother and if he'd loved her terribly and how it had felt to be in love.

Her own emotions were in a mess. She was excited and happy one minute, miserable and lonely the next. Jon had been right to pull back. There was no way they could maintain a light and casual affair. Things were too intense between them.

And she could never give him the family he deserved.

After the ten o'clock news, she brushed her teeth, turned out the lights, then lingered by the large window in the family room and gazed out at the night.

The moon was glorious, so full and heavy, she wanted to reach out and pluck it from the sky like a piece of lush, exotic fruit.

She wished Jon were there to watch it with her.

Jon walked the path between the fields until he stood by the creek that ran into the Sabine River a couple of miles farther down the road. The restlessness was with him again.

He thought of Anne. The full moon had a golden overlay to its silvery beauty. It reminded him of her smooth, satiny skin.

Except the moon looked cold. She would be warm.

Warm and welcoming. She'd indicated she wanted him, no strings attached. It was damned unnerving.

He sighed. He couldn't sleep and hadn't for a week, it seemed. Why should he torture himself when bliss was apparently his for the taking? Anne lived only a few miles away. He gazed down the road, wondering if she would welcome him....

Going to the truck, he climbed in and started the engine. He let it idle for a moment, then feeling his fate was sealed, he put it into gear and drove the few miles into town. He parked in the courthouse lot and walked the short block back.

He stopped at the edge of the school yard and peered across the street at her house. Disappointment bit into him.

Her windows were dark, the house silent.

Pondering his next action, he stuck his hands in his back pockets and rocked back on his heels, indecision eating at him.

At that moment, the front door opened and Anne, ethereal in a long nightgown, stepped onto the porch. She stood there, watching him watch her.

The moonlight gilded her so that she looked like an angel. Not exactly the image he wanted. His body quickened, and heat surged from deep inside to warm him against the cool night.

One step. Another. He was in the street. Down the road, car lights swung across him as a car left the gas station, then went in the opposite direction. He continued his journey.

At the bottom of the steps, he hesitated, not sure what he'd be committing himself to if he climbed those two stairs.

"Step into my parlor," she said. Her voice was soft, her tone light and reassuring, but throbbing with things he couldn't name, only feel.

He realized she'd read his doubts as clearly as if she'd peered into his head. "Are you the spider and I the fly…or is the opposite true?" He heard the deepened timbre, the faint tremolo of his own voice and knew that he was surely caught.

"We're moonstruck. Haven't you heard of that brand of madness? It's brief, but oh, so glorious." She laughed, an almost inaudible ripple of invitation.

There was a tinge of stubbornness in her tone, as if she wouldn't be denied her whimsical moment. She took his hand and led him up the steps, across the silver-glazed porch and into her house. His heart beat very fast, very hard.

He closed the door behind them and laid his hands on her shoulders. He had to make one more attempt at being honorable. "This isn't right for you. You live here. Your neighbors will gossip about us."

She dismissed his worries. "They gossip about everybody."

"You're not the type to have a casual affair."

"I don't intend for it to be casual." She caressed his face with the gentlest of touches. "Passionate, yes. Casual, no."

His gallantry evaporated with the warmth of her caress. "It must be madness," he murmured, pulling her into his arms and inhaling deeply. The scent of her hair and skin was so enticing, he closed his eyes to savor it better.

"Moonstruck madness," she agreed, curving into him as gracefully as a swan glides upon water.

"Anne," he growled, gut-deep and yearning. "I don't want to frighten you...." A tremor went through him as he held himself back.

"You won't." Her hands soothed him, rubbing over his shoulders and through his hair. It was oddly comforting.

"I want to eat you up, to soak into you until neither of us knows where one begins and the other ends."

"Oh, Jon, that's incredibly beautiful."

He drew back. "You," he murmured. "You're beautiful."

With careful intent, he explored her through the knitted material of her nightgown. "Let's get out of the parlor and into the bedroom," he suggested. "My knees are getting weak."

She nipped him through his T-shirt, then spun away, racing along the hall. "Catch me."

He followed at a fast pace, but not running. There would be no rushing this night, he vowed. He'd go slow with her....

When she paused at an open door to glance back, he caught her hair, kissed the lock, then swept her into his arms. Feeling like a conquering hero, he carried her inside.

Moonlight flooded the room. He made his way across the floor, avoiding the footstool in front of a granny rocker.

He wanted to see her, but this light was enough for the first time. When they were at ease with each other, then he'd ask for light. He placed her on the bed, bracing one knee on the mattress as he lowered her.

The covers were already turned down. The bedspread was neatly folded at the foot of the bed. Surprise made him smile.

"Queen-size," he murmured. "I hadn't expected such luxury from a woman alone."

"My father gave it to me. I think he thought of it as part of my dowry."

"Mmm."

"But I don't."

He sat beside her and stroked her lean, surprisingly firm body from neck to knees, then glided back to her chest. She had nice breasts, neither big nor small. A comfortable handful of womanly flesh. He smiled.

"What?" she demanded, smiling back.

"You. Just . . . you."

"You make me feel incredibly beautiful . . . and irresistibly sexy." She arched against his hand, sending shards of sensation up his arm and down his chest to lodge in the pit of his stomach.

"May I?" He reached down to the hem of her gown.

"Yes, please," she said politely.

He slipped the cotton up past her knees and onto her thighs. She lifted her hips. Using both hands, he quickly pushed it to her waist. With a graceful move, she sat up and held her arms over her head, making it easy for him to complete the task. He tossed the garment onto the rocking chair.

Then he simply stared at her.

Her body was alabaster pale in the moon-brightened room, all except for the delicate darkness guarding the fragile curve of her womanly mons. His heart constricted as tenderness washed over him.

"Woman, thy name is Anne," he whispered, reverent and shaken by the wonder of her.

She ran her hands over his chest. "Kiss me," she ordered. "I want to see if it's as wonderful as I remember."

He complied, swooping to her waiting lips with a sureness he was far from feeling. He sought the inner treasure. Her mouth was sweet with the lingering mint of toothpaste.

For every kiss he gave, she gave one back, her mouth moving over his as eagerly as he explored hers. It was a wild coming together of passion and other things, things he couldn't begin to describe. He tried to go slow, to be careful.

When he came up for air, she moaned and murmured his name. He'd never known the sound of his name on a woman's lips could be so arousing.

He was hard and pulsing with life. He knew in another time, another place, he would have planted his seed in her without regard to the consequences, knowing only that he had to have her.

But not in this time, this place.

There was her future and her reputation to consider. As a lover, he meant everything about their coupling to be perfect for her, with no worries or regrets in the morning.

Easing away, he silenced her protest, then began kissing her neck. He breathed deeply of the sweet scent of her body. Her aroma was of shampoo and soap, of powder and cologne and the personal perfume that was uniquely hers.

Kissing her along her breast, he found one tiny nipple and felt it contract further as he laved it with his tongue. He felt her catch her breath, then let it out in a swoosh of delight.

He had to explore further. His hunger raged now, and he had to sample all of her. He ran his tongue around her navel and felt her muscles clench. He chuckled, knowing he could produce a response wherever he touched.

Lower, he brushed his face from side to side, liking the feel of the soft curls against his skin.

"Jon?" she said.

For the first time, he detected a slight nervousness in her. They were new to each other as lovers, and he realized she was reticent about this most intimate of kissing.

He paused. "It's all right, love. If you don't enjoy it, I'll stop. I promise," he added. He bent to her again, stroking that incredible smoothness until she trembled and, unable to help herself, began to move to the rhythm of his caresses.

He delighted in the taste of her, the earthy delicacy, the womanly sweetness he found in the soft folds of her flesh.

When she whimpered in need, he pressed harder, unable to stop as she cried out and clutched at him wildly. He wanted this for her... his gift... pure... with no taking... only giving...

"Come to me," she cried in soft gasps. "Come to me. *Now.*"

When she quietened, he stood and started to remove his T-shirt. He stopped, remembering what he'd forgotten in the heat of passion.

"I can't," he murmured, lying with her and gathering her close. She clung to him in sweet contentment.

"You can't?"

He smiled at the confusion and disbelief in her tone. "I forgot to bring protection," he explained wryly. He thought briefly of the packets... still in the truck.

"Where's your truck?"

"Parked down the street."

"Why?" she demanded.

He realized she wasn't thinking of future consequences. "I shouldn't be seen here at this time of night."

As if the neighbors wouldn't see his truck near her house and come up with the correct assumption. She stroked down his body and laid her hand against the hard ridge trapped beneath his jeans. "You haven't been satisfied."

"Yes, I have. More than you'll ever know." He chuckled at her snort of disbelief. To have pleased her made him feel like the best lover in the universe.

"We owe it to Dave to try those snuggies and see if they're any good. Why don't you go get them?" she proposed.

He groaned. "I've created a monster." He pushed himself up from her and adjusted his jeans to a slightly more comfortable position. He started for the door. He'd better leave before he forgot his good intentions. "Don't marry the senator," he advised. "Wait for the man who can make you feel what I just did. There'll be someone for you."

She didn't answer.

He walked out, remembering Bogie at the end of *Casablanca,* knowing this was the way it had to be and feeling like hell.

Anne stood by the telephone. At last she picked it up and dialed Jon's number. He answered on the second ring, his voice thick and sexy. She realized her call had awakened him.

Little tingles dashed along her chest as she thought of sleeping with him, of waking in the morning...

"Hello?" he said again.

She pushed herself out of the daydream. "Good morning. This is Anne. I need to ask a favor. I have a wedding this morning and I need more flowers. I was wondering if you could deliver the rest of my Christmas poinsettia order now—those that have the most color showing."

There was a dead silence on the line. Finally he spoke. "How many do you need?"

"Twenty or thirty pots."

"Okay. I'll get them loaded and be there within an hour. Where do you want them delivered?"

"At my shop. The church is across the street. Come by my house first. I'll have breakfast ready." She hung up.

Her hands trembled ever so little as she prepared bacon and waffles. Everything was ready by the time she heard his truck turn in at her drive. "Come in. The door's open," she called when his step sounded on the porch.

He entered with a cautious air. She gave him a bright smile to show there were no hard feelings about last night. He relaxed as he took the chair she indicated. "You're feeling chipper this morning," he commented, giving her a close scrutiny.

"Yes, I am." She refrained from asking him if he'd had a bad night. He obviously had. "I appreciate your doing this. The bride's mother wanted me to use the flowers from her garden, but they weren't ready. She was about to have a hissy fit until I remembered the poinsettias."

He nodded at her explanation and began eating when she did.

"You're one of the most unpredictable females I ever met," Jon grumbled when she paused in her chatter about the wedding.

"How's that?"

"You should be thinking of ways to get me to the altar. It's a female's natural right."

"And what's the male's natural right?"

"To resist." He grinned at her.

"There's no need for all that controversy. We can both enjoy the moment. There'll be no hard feelings when it's over. At least I hope there won't." She gazed at him solemnly.

"Dammit, Anne," he said softly, exasperated with her casual air about the whole thing.

"What?" Her eyes were as innocent as a lamb's.

"You're not taking this with the . . . the proper seriousness." He sounded like a Victorian prig.

"Where is it written that the female has to be left behind, weeping and gnashing her teeth, when an affair is over?"

This was not the way things went between men and women in his experience. Woman tried to find ways to trap a man—with sex, kids or financial dependence. They did not blithely smile while conducting an affair in front of their entire hometown.

"This must be a new angle. Don't worry. I'll catch on."

She smiled, shook her head and settled down to eating the delicious meal. He ate, too, but not with his usual enjoyment.

Things just didn't add up here. She wasn't acting right. It irritated the hell out of him trying to figure it out.

"Here's the paper. I think I'll change for the ceremony now. I'm running out of time," she remarked, putting her dishes in the dishwasher a few minutes later. "You can drop me by the shop and unload the flowers there."

"The shop." His voice broke on the word and fluted into a tenor he hadn't had since he'd passed puberty. "If someone sees us, they might get the wrong idea. My truck was near here last night, then if we're seen together this early in the morning—"

"Really, Jon, you're too much."

Still shaking her head, she headed for the bedroom, leaving him with the Monday paper to read. He tried to concentrate on world affairs, but they paled in interest beside his own.

When she returned, looking like an angel in a pale yellow dress with a lacy jacket over it, he silently rose and escorted her to the truck. "You're pretty dressed up for work. Is the senator coming for the wedding?"

"Jealous?"

"Yes."

"Good. And no, he's not. Let's go."

A dangerous word—*wedding*, he thought as he drove the short distance to her shop. Women went soft at the mention of it. Men found themselves caught before they knew it. He parked, went around the truck and swung her down to the pavement, getting a nice glimpse of thigh as a reward. His temperature rose.

A drowning sensation hit him. He recognized the signs of incipient softheadedness. He'd better get out of—

"Good morning. Glad to see you're joining us," one of the local preachers called out, beaming a stock-in-trade hundred-watt smile on them as he crossed the street. "It's good that Anne has a strong young fellow like you to help her out," he boomed out so half the town could hear. "You'll enjoy the service."

"I, uh, I'm not dressed . . . for a wedding," he hastily added. "I'm here to help with the flowers." He felt sweat pop out on his forehead and wondered if his words, although true, sounded as false to the preacher as they did to him.

Anne gave him a wry glance. Her impish humor laughed at him from her gorgeous eyes. For a minute he thought she was going to deny his statement, but she ducked into her store and left him on the sidewalk with the minister.

"I wanted to thank you for your help," the man continued. "Anne said you donated a number of plants equal to what the beautification committee bought. It's good for the community to see the generosity of young people like yourself. And Anne, of course. She's a wonder, isn't she?''

"Uh, yes." Jon's thoughts went to the night just past and the hour he'd held her and nearly made love... well, he *had* made love to her, but not to completion. He'd dreamed of her....

"Well, I'd better run." The preacher headed for the trim brick church.

Jon moved his truck to the side door of the chapel and started unloading the poinsettias. He had the task done before Anne reappeared. He jumped inside the pickup and cranked up. Before he drove off, he saw Anne leave her shop and go to the church. She looked like a flower in her yellow dress. She waved to him before he was out of sight.

She was special, he mused. And she deserved someone just as special. That someone wasn't him no matter how much he might dream of the two of them settling down to married bliss on the ranch, raising pines and cows and flowers and kids...

Anne looked the church over, a satisfied smile on her face. Lina and she had covered the poinsettia pots with white foil to reflect the winter wedding theme and placed them on the steps at either side of the altar.

The church was filling quickly now. One thing the townfolk loved was a ceremony. Weddings ran neck and neck with funerals in popularity.

"What's this I hear about Jon Sinclair being at your house last night and this morning?" a voice demanded behind Anne.

Startled, she glanced around and found Ellen smiling at her in open approval. She smiled in welcome. "Well, that much is true, but he wasn't there for the hours between."

She wondered which of her neighbors had seen Jon enter her house last night and had reported the news.

"He wasn't?" Ellen was frankly disappointed.

Anne shook her head and slipped into a seat. "He was a true gentleman, properly concerned about my reputation in a town filled with nosy people." She looked pointedly at her friend.

Ellen sat beside her. "Heck," she muttered.

"Nothing is going to happen between Jon Sinclair and myself," she informed Ellen. "He's a friend, nothing more."

"Tell me another one before that one gets cold." Ellen gave her a puzzled glance. "I don't understand you."

Anne's aunt arrived, interrupting the conversation. After she'd exchanged pleasantries, she leaned close to Anne. "It's all over town that the Sinclair boy spent the night at your house."

Anne felt her hackles rise at her aunt's furious tone. It made her want to add something outrageous to the gossip floating around town about them. "He's not a boy," she said, keeping her voice low. "He's a man."

Aunt Marge gasped and turned an interesting shade of purple. "Really, Anne, what are you thinking of—"

"He didn't spend the night," Anne broke in, sorry that she'd allowed her tongue to get away from her. "Your informant should have told you he left at a respectable hour, before midnight, actually."

Ellen leaned around Anne and whispered so Marge could hear. "You shouldn't have let him get away. If ever a man was ready for a home and family, it's Jon Sinclair."

Marge glared at Ellen. Ellen smiled blithely. Anne felt like the referee in a boxing match. "But I'm not," she said to her friend and watched surprise darken Ellen's eyes while Aunt Marge's gleamed in triumph.

Neither of them knew what an effort it cost her to say the words. It was getting harder to think of Jon as a temporary lover...and dangerous to think of him as anything else.

An expectant shuffling brought everyone's attention to the front. The minister, the groom and the best man took their places. The mothers were escorted to their seats. The notes of "The Wedding March" wafted clear and golden from the organ.

Anne's throat constricted as she stood and watched the solemn bride walk down the aisle with her equally solemn father.

For a moment, she visualized herself in a white dress, her hand on her father's arm as she walked toward her love...

Before the imaginary groom could turn toward her, she wiped the picture from her mind, suddenly afraid to see his face, afraid it would belong to the wrong man.

But who was the right one? her heart demanded to know.

She had no answer.

7

"Would you mind asking him?"

Anne smothered her irritation. The Civic Improvement Committee wanted her to ask Jon if they could host a fund-raiser at his place for the new gym.

"A tour of the gardens would be perfect and the spring flowers will be in full bloom," the pastor's wife continued.

"I'll ask," Anne heard herself say and wondered if she'd completely lost her mind. She hadn't seen hide nor hair of Jon Sinclair since he'd left her Monday morning. Four days.

"I knew we could count on you." The woman stood and smoothed her skirt. She opened her mouth, closed it, then opened it again. "Anne, dear..."

"Yes?" A frisson shivered down her back.

"Do be careful, won't you?"

Anne felt heat seep into her ears. "Of course." She smiled brightly. "I always watch both ways when crossing the street."

Mrs. Copeland hesitated, then patted Anne's arm. With a murmur of farewell, she hurried off to complete the list of saintly duties expected of a preacher's wife.

Ellen laughed. "Crossing the street—that was a good one."

Anne sighed. "Everyone in town has advised me."

"You sound glum. Where's Jon been this week?"

"You tell me. I haven't seen him since Monday when he dropped me at work, then skedaddled out of town."

"I never thought he'd turn out to be a coward."

Anne glared at her best friend. "He isn't. He thinks he's bad for me, so he's leaving me alone. I think."

Ellen's eyebrows shot up. She leaned forward eagerly. "Really? Did he say that?"

"He advised me not to marry Randall, also that someone would come along for me who would make me feel—" She stopped, not wanting to reveal more.

"It was wonderful between you two, huh?" Ellen sighed dreamily. "I wish someone would come along and sweep me off my feet, make me faint dead away and not take no for an answer."

"Come on," Anne chided. "You've been in love with Doc for ages. You wouldn't recognize Prince Charming if he ran over you with his white charger."

"I might." Ellen's expression changed to mulish.

"Hmm, maybe Doc needs some competition to wake him up to what he's missing. My dad's coming home soon."

"Oh, sure, a big businessman who has his pick of the world's beauties would be overwhelmed by a small-town spinster like me."

Anne shrugged. "He hasn't married one of those beauties." She stood. "Well, I suppose I'd better get over to the shop. Lina wants to leave early for a big date with Steve. I hope I haven't opened a can of worms with those two."

Ellen picked right up on her worries. "Her father and brothers don't want her seeing anyone. They're afraid to let her go. Who else would put up with them?"

"Why *do* women put up with slobs like that? What do we need men for, anyway?" She left money on the table and walked out of the restaurant. Ellen's laughter wafted behind her, which was the effect she'd been aiming for.

Ellen had taken over Doc's office after his wife died, but she hadn't taken over his heart. Not yet. Maybe Doc did need some friendly competition. She'd ask Jon for his opinion when she asked about using his place for the barbecue.

Ellen followed her to the flower shop. They found Lina in tears in the back room. "Hey, what's wrong?" Anne asked. She'd never seen Lina show any emotion during the two years she'd been working there. It took a few minutes, but Ellen coaxed the problem from her.

Her brothers had informed her father that she was seeing Steve. They'd embroidered the story a bit, saying Steve was a womanizer and a troublemaker. Her father had forbidden her to see the young man again.

"Wait a minute," Ellen said. "You're over twenty-one, and this isn't the Dark Ages. Where does he get off, telling you who you can see?"

"He's impossible to deal with," Lina said, still weeping.

"What does Steve say?"

"I haven't told him yet. He's supposed to pick me up here in a few minutes."

Ellen handed out advice. "Let him handle it. After all, he's the one with the bad reputation. He should be the one to defend himself. Tell him what your brothers said. He'll know what to do."

When the young man arrived, Lina rushed to him. They went outside and sat in his truck. Anne observed Lina's gestures and deduced the younger woman was explaining the situation. When Steve looked furious, she was sure of it.

"Ha!" Ellen said as if things were moving right along as she'd wanted them to.

In a few minutes, Steve put Lina out and took off in a cloud of burning rubber.

"Oh, help," Lina called as she burst into the shop. "Steve is going to beat my brothers up, then talk to my father."

"Good. They'll have this straightened out in no time." Ellen smiled brightly. "Well, now that we've taken care of Lina's problem, let's work on Anne's."

"I don't have a problem," Anne spoke up, afraid of what Ellen had in mind for her.

"Oh, yes, you do. You don't know it yet."

"You're my problem. Are you going to provoke a fight with Jon next? Who's going to be his opponent?"

"Randall."

Anne groaned at the gleeful snicker from her friend. "Back off," she warned, "else the town is going to have a new subject to talk about—mainly, your demise."

Ellen ignored her. "I think pistols at dawn on Main Street would be the perfect romantic setup. They can duel over you."

"Jon would shoot into the ground. He's already scared he might get stuck with me."

"Hmm, we'll have to work on that boy."

Lina brightened up at the banter between the other two. By the time the store closed, she was angry with men in general and with her relatives and sweetheart in particular.

Steve hadn't returned. A call to her home disclosed that he and her brothers were sitting on the front porch, talking about hunting dogs. "Steve-a-roo is all right," her father reported.

"They're sitting out there drinking beer and exchanging stories," Lina fumed to her friends, "while I worried about them."

"They aren't worth it," Ellen declared.

"Right."

"Let's go somewhere, just us girls, and have some fun."

"Let's," Lina agreed, her usual sweet nature overturned by anger with Steve.

"I know just the place," Ellen decided.

Anne peered at the determined faces of the other two. She sensed trouble brewing. Ellen was feeling rambunctious and Lina was in the mood for revenge. "I'll drive," she said.

She taped a note on the door in case the errant boyfriend decided to reappear for his date. Lina and Ellen opposed the idea but Anne won out.

She drove out to the restaurant near the coast called the Roadhouse, which was famed for its beer-battered shrimp. The noise from the jukebox blasted their ears when they opened the heavy oak door.

"Yeah, this is the way I remember it," Ellen shouted. "It's good to know some things never change."

Anne hadn't been there since a bunch of high school friends had dared each other to go. The night had ended in a fight.

The place looked ready for another one. It was filled with sailors from a local fishing fleet, a construction crew and a few real cowboys, who were minding their own business.

There were three men for each woman, Anne calculated. Not bad odds. After their meal, one of the local cowboys, who knew Ellen, ambled over. He asked to be introduced, then promptly invited Anne to dance.

She declined. "My bum knee is acting up."

He turned to Lina, who went to the dance floor with him. Anne watched them with a worried frown. "Oh-oh."

"He's okay," Ellen said. "I know him."

"That's not the problem. Steve and Lina's brothers just walked in."

Ellen twisted around and peered through the smoke and gloom toward the front door. Steve and two beefy guys shoved their way inside. A fourth man followed them.

"Well, this makes it perfect," Ellen declared.

Jon spotted the women, spoke to the other three and pushed his way toward their table. "What are you doing here?" he yelled at Anne, a definite frown on his handsome face.

"Eating," she yelled back. "They have the best shrimp."

He looked exasperated. She gave him a bland smile. Who asked him to show up and be a wet blanket?

She faced forward in time to see Steve cut in on Lina's dancing partner. Lina refused to dance with him. One of the sailors took umbrage when Steve tried to insist she leave the crowded floor. Her brothers snarled at the sailor. The sailor's friends decided he'd been insulted.

As Anne had expected—a tussle was about to start.

"Stay put," Jon ordered. He rescued Lina from the milling masculine bodies, then swept the three women before him as if herding chickens to their roost. Once he had them outside, he went back in for Steve and the two brothers.

Five minutes later, he reappeared with the men. He wiped blood from the corner of his mouth with a handkerchief. Steve looked contrite.

"I accidentally hit him," he explained when Anne went to Jon and asked about his injury. "I thought he was one of the other men when he touched my shoulder."

"It was a glancing blow," Jon assured her. "It's nothing." He glared at the three women. "When Steve called to say you were here, I couldn't believe it. What the hell was that all about?" He gestured to the noisy restaurant.

"We just wanted to have some fun," Anne quipped, angry at herself for worrying about him. The brute hadn't called her once all week.

"Well, playtime is over. You're going home." He clasped her arm and tried to guide her into his truck.

Behind them, Steve hustled Lina into his pickup. Ellen ducked into the back seat of a tiny compact. The two burly brothers got into the front. Anne wondered why the tires didn't sag. Both groups drove off, leaving her and Jon.

"Get in," he said.

"I have my car."

"Have you been drinking?" He eyed her suspiciously and bent forward to sniff her breath.

"No. Not that it's any of your business if I have."

"You're not acting your usual self," he muttered with a worried frown. "Let's go home, then we'll talk. I'll follow."

He saw her safely to her car, then fell in behind her for the twenty-minute trip to her house. There, he pulled into the drive and waited while she entered and closed the garage, then went into her house, flipping on lights as she hurried to the side door to let him in.

The moon wasn't as full as the previous weekend, but it still cast a bright glow over the landscape. Jon sat in his truck. She could see his hands gripping the steering wheel and sensed the battle he fought with himself over her.

"Make up your mind," she called out. "Either go or stay, but don't just sit there."

He slammed out of the truck. She stepped aside when he came inside and closed the door none too gently. "You're enough to make a saint swear," he informed her.

"Well, you're certainly not one of those." She stuck her hands on her hips and gave him glare for glare.

That seemed to surprise him. "What were you doing at a dive like that at this time of the night?"

"Watching out for my two best friends." She bestowed a facetious smile on him.

"You're in a strange mood."

"Am I? Maybe I'm just tired of men making all the rules and taking advantage of women."

"Men taking advantage of women," he repeated with an incredulous expression. "Who went to dinner at a place known for trouble at nine o'clock at night? And who was the stupid oaf that rescued you?"

She placed a finger under her chin as if in deep thought. "Oh, let me see if I can figure it out. I got it—Red Riding Hood and the Lone Ranger."

He was clearly taken aback at her manner. He grasped her by the shoulders. "This isn't like you."

It wasn't, but she was tired of being nice. She was tired of acting cheerful so Aunt Marge and Uncle Joe and the whole town wouldn't worry about her. She was tired of his come-hither-go-away attitude. Most of all, she was tired of fighting the attraction between them.

The silence spun golden webs of longing around them. Her anger disappeared. The urge to touch him grew. When she could no longer resist, she leaned her head to the side and stroked the back of his hand with her cheek.

"Anne," he warned in a throaty murmur.

"No," she whispered, "no lectures."

"This isn't the answer. Passion doesn't solve anything. It complicates the situation. Surely you can see that."

"Yes, I see all the complications." The complications of falling in love, of wanting more than she could ever have. She straightened. "How's your thumb?" she asked politely.

He held up his left hand. He wore a bandage over the end of his thumb. "It's fine." He sighed. "Why do I want you more than food or water or air? What kind of spell is this?"

She had no answer.

He closed his arms around her and rested his chin on her head as he thought things over. "If we have an affair, how can I be sure it won't harm you?"

"Or you. Will you be able to go away and forget what happened between us?"

She felt his chest lift and drop in a sigh. "Some things a man doesn't want to forget. You're definitely one of them."

"So are you."

"Why are you determined to marry an older man?"

She extricated herself from his embrace. Going into the kitchen, she put on coffee and sliced a cake her aunt had sent over the day before. She talked as she worked. "You remember my steady from college?"

"The one you were almost engaged to?"

"Yes. We had decided to get married, but while on a visit to his parents to break the news, I realized he and his whole family would expect more of me than I wanted to give."

"So you backed off," he mused. "Were they high society?"

"Yes, the cream of Philadelphia."

"Lots of good works, charity functions and all that?"

"Exactly."

"So what's different about that from what you're doing now? Or what you'd be doing as the senator's wife?"

"I get to choose my own pet projects." She wrinkled her nose at him as she plunked plates, forks and cups on the table. Jon poured the coffee while she fetched napkins.

When they were seated, he stared at her thoughtfully. She detected suspicion, wariness and concern in his eyes. She braced herself for more questions.

"You worry me," he admitted.

"You and my aunt should get together. You can discuss where I'm going wrong in my life."

"This isn't funny. By the way, the man at the quick market told me not to let your aunt scare me off."

The longing increased along with her heart rate. "It seems that lots of folks are determined I'm going to have a love life, no matter what Aunt Marge does to discourage it."

"Why is she against your dating? I don't think she likes the senator, either."

Anne scooped up the last bite of cake and ate it before answering. "She doesn't. She thinks marriage will be too hard on me. She's helped raise me since I was a baby. She's afraid for me."

"Because of your heart?"

"Yes. My uncle explained it to me after she and I had a quarrel one time. They lost two children soon after birth. I'm all she has left. Besides my uncle, of course."

"So you had to fight to have your own life. Maybe that's why you're afraid to marry." His silvery eyes narrowed as he studied her. "Don't marry Randall. He isn't right for you. There'll be someone else."

It was clear he didn't see himself as that person. "Are you turning into a marriage counselor?" she demanded, striving for the distance that raillery would put between them.

"I suppose. Since you've conceived this great passion for me, I feel obligated to help you find your soul mate."

An odd expression crossed his face, then was gone. She hadn't been able to read it, but it was something that startled him out of his complacent—and irritating—paternalism.

"Don't bother." She poured them fresh coffee. He cleared the table and put away the used plates and forks. "You're very domesticated for a hardened bachelor."

"My mom believed people should clean up after themselves. She was one of the original feminists. My father held the same ideals. They both marched in freedom parades and worked for equal rights for all people."

"Really?"

He nodded. "They were brilliant thinkers, but neither knew the first thing about business and money. I found them to be exasperating at times."

"Why didn't you follow in their footsteps?"

"I opted to see the world instead. Actually, when things were going well at the chicken factory, I did take some business courses in college. I didn't go back after the first couple of years. I knew more about business than the professors."

"Nothing like a humble attitude."

"The courses were for bean counters. I had already learned you only needed to be tougher than the guys you were dealing with in order to win."

His lessons on life hadn't destroyed his innate honesty or goodness. "Tough... and brilliant, too," she mocked gently.

"Sorry. I didn't mean to come on as the world's greatest know-it-all."

"You didn't," she said. "You're a very nice person. Tough as you had to be, maybe, but fair, too. The fire chief *and* his sons have been singing your praises all week. I think there's a soft spot in your heart for troublesome kids."

He carried his cup to the dishwasher and tucked it in the rack. "Don't be fooled. I gave them a job to impress you, because I wanted in your bed."

"Blunt and to the point," she murmured, dredging up a dose of humor. "I like that in a man. It makes life simpler."

"Hell, nothing has been simple since I met you. Next thing I know you'll have me doing do-gooder stuff."

"Now that you mention it..."

"Oh, no." He headed toward the door.

She beat him to it and blocked his way with arms spread to either side and hands clutching the frame. "The pastor's wife is in charge of the gym fund-raising project. She wants to use your place for a cookout in the spring. She needs to plan it now."

He stopped an inch from her. "Is that all?"

"And a tour of the gardens at ten dollars a person."

"A tour and a cookout?"

"And maybe a dance afterward in that lovely huge garden room at your house. The committee will take care of the arrangements. You won't have to do a thing."

"A tour, a cookout and a dance," he counted up. "What do I get out of this?"

"My eternal gratitude?" She rose on tiptoe and kissed him quite gently on the chin.

He groaned and slipped his arms around her. "You know better than to tempt me like that."

"No, I don't."

"Yes, you do."

"I don't." She kissed him again.

"You do." He held her tighter.

"Don't." She let him take part of her weight.

"Do." He kissed her—once, hard and hungry—then he left her like all hell was after him.

She sighed. It was going to be a beautiful affair. She just had to remember to keep both feet on the ground.

Jon stood on the patio outside the terrace room. The air was a pleasant sixty-eight degrees with a wonderful crispness to it that invigorated the mind and spirit. Clouds played hide-and-seek with the sun.

He studied the sky. A storm was gathering.

Another was brewing inside him. Anne was coming to his place after she closed her shop. This was a planning session for the fund-raiser she had mentioned the previous night. She'd called that morning and asked if she could check things over.

Saturday. Two weeks since the kiss that had started this whole affair... not affair... They were not having an affair.

His breath caught as a sharp ache penetrated his chest. He hadn't invited her to have dinner with him, but he already had a salad made, steaks marinating, ready for the grill, and wine cooling in the fridge. Everything a fellow needed for seduction.

A groan rumbled deep inside him. Maybe she'd look the place over and leave. That would be best. If he didn't see her, he might get over the insane idea that he had to have her, that his personal happiness depended on her.

It didn't.

Another jolt went through him when he spied a car coming up the gravel road to the house. Yes, it was she.

The corner of the house blocked her from view as she drove up the curving drive and parked at the front.

He went down the steps and around the house, intending to meet her and welcome her with something stupid like, "Welcome to my castle."

The Ralston boys beat him to it. When he arrived at the front of the house, they were ten steps ahead of him.

They yanked the car door open and, both talking at once, regaled her with the big happening of the day.

"Jon and me were working in the potting shed..."

"I was in one of the greenhouses with Pedro..."

"And I picked up a one-gallon pot..."

"When we heard Jase hollering like mad..."

"It had a yellow jacket's nest inside. I dropped..."

"Me and Pedro ran outside. Jon told us to go back. There were wasps all—"

"It's my story," Jase said with a frown toward his younger brother, then turned back to Anne. "I dropped the pot. It caused the wasps to swarm—"

"And they were trying to bite him," Teddy broke in.

Jase gave him a frown. "Wasps don't bite. They *sting*. And one of them did sting me." He held up his forearm to show her the wound.

She admired it and commented on his bravery. "I'm surprised more of them didn't get you."

"Jon turned the water hose on them. Every time one came at us, he sprayed it down on the ground, then stomped it. He told me to go to the greenhouse, but I stayed and helped. He wet 'em down and I stomped 'em good."

"I would have helped," Teddy spoke up, "but Pedro said we'd better not get in the way."

"Jon said if you kept spit on the sting, it would make the hurt go away faster. And guess what? It worked," Jase ended on a proud note.

"Well, that was certainly an adventure," Anne commented at the end of the story.

Jon felt his insides burn to cinders at her approving smile. Every good intention he'd had toward her disappeared in the heat.

"Are you okay? Did you get stung?" she asked, coming up the walk toward him, her young admirers at each side.

He shook his head.

The wind kicked up at that moment, causing her hair to swirl around her shoulders like a silk cape, dark and mysterious in its shiny black depths, magic stuff that enchanted him.

"There's the truck. Pedro is driving us home. See ya tomorrow after our scout meeting, Jon. Bye, Anne."

The brothers raced each other to the pickup. First one there got the window seat while the other had to sit in the middle. Jon noticed that Jase let his younger brother win today.

"How are they doing?" Anne asked him when the truck headed down the drive.

"Fine. They're good kids, all heart once you get past their curiosity. That's mostly why they pull pranks. They want to see what will happen."

"I think they've learned to think ahead lately."

He feasted on her slender legs and hips as she walked toward him. She wore black slacks with a blue knit top. Her sandals were black with big blue fake jewels on them. She wore earrings with matching gemstones.

She looked cool and collected while he felt sweaty-palmed and shaky-kneed.

"The terrace room is this way." He gestured in the general direction and stepped aside to let her precede him.

"Is that the garden room with all the sliding glass doors your mother had built for her orchids?"

"Yes."

"Are you using it now?"

"Come and see."

She tucked her hand into the crook of his arm so that he had no choice but to walk beside her, their hips brushing once in a while as they rounded the house.

"Oh," she breathed, peering at the glass-walled room. She released him and raced ahead, entering through the doors he'd left open. "This is perfect."

He glanced around the spacious room. The terrazzo floor was polished to a high shine. The embedded marble chips were green and gold. Orchids lined the side that adjoined the house. A fountain of flowing water ran around half the perimeter, forming a tiny creek. Ferns and orchids lined its banks.

"This could be used on a movie set. I can see the beautiful people dancing here. Cocktails and food would be served over there. A small dance band would fit on the steps."

Her pleasure was reflected in her face. He watched while she curtsied to an imaginary partner, then began to waltz, humming to herself as she did. He gritted his teeth and looked away. But not for long.

When she came near him, she smiled and held out her arms.

He took the two steps that would put him in dance position with her. They danced around the room to the tune she hummed.

When she stopped humming, he dipped her backward until her hair brushed the terrazzo, then brought her upright.

Her breasts grazed his chest, searing him with the need to touch her. His breath quickened. He felt a tremor run over her. Slowly, as if in a dream, he drew her close.

She licked her lips. He stared at them hungrily.

"Anne," he said. He wasn't sure if it was an entreaty or a protest. Some of both.

For a moment, they stood there like statues. Time lost all meaning as he gazed into her eyes. She sighed as if saddened beyond words at some thought, then smiled.

"You must have loved it here," she said. She stepped out of his arms. "Growing up in such lovely surroundings."

"It was okay. I had the place pretty much to myself. I used to wonder why my mother wanted this area enclosed. It was the original patio. She and my father were always busy reading or writing letters to newspapers or the president. They rarely entertained guests or came outside."

She turned those incredibly sexy eyes on him. "Was it lonely for you? I get the impression they were more interested in their causes than their son or the ranch."

He realized Anne looked beneath the surface to the heart of things. He hadn't meant to give that much of himself away.

"I had Pedro," he said. "He let me help him with the chores around here. Sometimes he took me home, and I'd share a holiday with his family. He and his wife had four kids."

"I know them. Steve's the youngest and has been the biggest problem for them, I think. How's he doing?"

"He hasn't been late for work once since you hooked him up with Lina. He'll be a married man in no time."

The idea hit Jon like a sledgehammer. Marriage? Was that what *he* was thinking of?

"Shall we check out the gardens?" he invited quickly, cutting off the thought.

"Yes. You must have a green thumb. Everything looks wonderful. I want to see my Christmas poinsettias. They are ready, aren't they?" They'd be used for the country club doings held from Christmas through New Year's Eve. The club was her biggest customer.

"Yes. Pedro has been fussing over them like a mother with a newborn. They've had the exact amount of darkness and TLC to ensure they would develop their color on time."

She laughed and ran ahead of him, and he was reminded of his youth and the pleasure he'd once taken in small things. He picked up his speed and dashed to her side. Taking her hand, he led her to the rows of greenhouses, actually plastic shells supported on a metal framework. There, he pointed out the poinsettias he'd deliver to her next week.

"Very nice," she murmured, looking the plants over. Again he caught a flash of approval from those gorgeous eyes.

He tensed at the familiar surge of need in his body. He couldn't be around her two minutes without going off the deep end of desire. It was damned humiliating.

"Anne," he said again. This time the need was unmistakable.

"Let's look at the rest of the gardens," she said, quickly turning away from him.

He followed more slowly, wondering if she was running from him . . . and why it mattered so much.

8

Anne stood on the bluff over the creek and watched the cows in the field below. Beyond the pastures, pine trees lined up in stately rows as far as the eye could see. She'd been dismayed to learn they herded the cattle on all-terrain vehicles instead of horses. It was cheaper, Jon had explained.

Inhaling slowly, she filled her lungs to capacity. The air was cool and refreshing. It crackled with the ominous threat of the gathering storm, suffusing her with nervous energy.

"Looks like a storm is blowing in," Jon remarked.

"Yes." Her hair swirled in a banshee dance with each gust, stinging as it whiplashed across her face. She pivoted into the wind, and her hair blew straight back.

Jon touched her arm. "We'd better head in. It's a quarter mile to the house."

"Let's dance in the storm," she said, closing her eyes to slits against the wayward wind and lifting her arms to embrace it as her partner.

Jon caught her hand and tugged her down the incline to the gravel road. "Hurry. Here comes the rain."

She looked to where he pointed. "Yes, I see it."

The rain was a curtain of gray stampeding toward them out of the northwest. She imagined a herd of wild mustangs galloping toward them, ready to sweep her and Jon up and away to some magical land beyond the clouds.

He tugged her into a run. She went with him, laughing as the wind and the rain bore down on them, coming closer and closer. They ran faster.

She could hear the rain hitting the ground behind them. The first chilling drops struck her on the back. Her hair blew over her face, and the droplets hit her neck, causing a chill.

"Cold," she said, and laughed again, deliriously happy all of a sudden. It was as if the storm danced in her soul.

"We're almost there."

He guided her up the steps and into the terrace room, then closed the sliding glass doors behind them. Flushed and panting, she stopped and turned toward the wall of windows.

Jon's arm glided around her. Together they watched the rain lash the glass. A shiver chased down her back.

His arm tightened, but he didn't speak. She felt they were caught in an enchanted moment in time. She wanted it to last forever and ever and ever....

"Jon," she whispered, longing raging inside her, reflecting the storm outside the windows.

He turned them so that they were face-to-face and, resting his arms on her shoulders, laced his fingers behind her head. "Were you running from me or to me?"

His voice undercut the fierce pound of the rain and the jittery tinkle of the fountain. It reminded her of the quiet of a forest glade—mysterious, darkly appealing and oddly soothing.

"I..." The words stuck, and she couldn't get them out.

She wasn't sure what she was trying to say. Emotion rose in her, filling her with a wild clamoring like a thousand drums inside her skull. She shook her head slowly side to side as the yearning increased to a burning pain.

His eyes questioned, probing to her very soul. "To me or from me, Anne?" he asked again.

"To you," she confessed.

He swept her against his chest. "Thank God," he muttered. "I was afraid . . . if you don't want this . . ."

"I do." A romantic involvement may have been the last thing either of them had wanted, but it was inescapable.

He pressed his forehead to hers. "It's too damned strong. The need, the hunger, they overwhelm the senses."

"Yes."

"It's greater than anything I've ever known."

She thought he sounded confused, perhaps resentful. It didn't matter. Nothing mattered but the driving need that pushed her toward completion in his arms.

"Dangerous." He kissed along her temple, inching closer and closer to her mouth.

Shaking her wind-tossed hair back, she lifted her face, wanting his kiss on her mouth. "Love me," she whispered.

"How can I help it?" he asked on a rueful note.

His lips hovered over hers for a brief second as he stared into her eyes. She saw tenderness as well as desire reflected in those silvery depths. Other emotions tangled there, too, but those she couldn't read.

She uttered a low, impatient sound as her own need for him increased. Wrapping her arms around his shoulders, she pressed upward until all the spaces between them were gone.

She reveled in his strength when he caught her against him, and marveled at the passionate intensity between them at each provocative thrust of his tongue against hers.

It was irresistible, the strange pull between them. Lust? Love? She was afraid to put a name to it.

A shudder coursed through her, reaching right down to her soul. A warning from her sane self in this world gone mad?

Outside, the wind shrieked with demonic fury, and the rain slashed the windows without pause. A damp chill invaded her body, and she shivered again.

"Come," Jon said.

She followed him without question. He led her inside the modest mansion, across a stately hall and up the stairs to a bedroom with a masculine appearance.

A pair of boots lay on their sides beside a comfortable-looking recliner. A book was turned facedown on the lamp table next to the chair. A bowl on the walnut dresser held loose change, a couple of matchbooks and a comb.

His hands were gentle as he stripped her sandals, then the wet clothing from her and laid the slacks and top over a clothes valet to dry. After kicking off his shoes, he unbuttoned his shirt and tossed it aside. It landed on the arm of the chair, one sleeve trailing on the floor. His jeans followed.

Her breath caught as she took in the masculine grace of his form. He wasn't a brawny man, although his shoulders were wide and muscles rippled under the tanned expanse of his skin. He had the lithe smoothness of a cat, a man of sinuous strength and masterful poise.

His briefs were starkly white against his tan. Wiry hairs formed a halo effect around his legs as he stepped between her and the window, then reached behind her.

"May I?" he asked in a sensuously deep voice.

"Yes." She pulled her hair aside so he could reach the snap fastening easily.

He slipped the underclothes from her, then himself, before settling his hands on her hips and pulling her close again. Being with him like this, skin against skin, set bonfires of fiery desire raging in her blood.

When he waltzed them toward the bed, she went breathlessly to her fate, knowing that this was meant to be. He paused and skimmed the covers out of the way with the downward sweep of one hand, then he laid her gently on the sweet-smelling sheet.

Sitting beside her, he ran the knuckles of his right hand over her contracting nipple until it squeezed into a tight bud. He smiled at his handiwork.

"When you respond like that, it drives me right to the edge . . ." His voice trailed off.

She rose and threw her arms around him, pressing her face into the hollow between his neck and shoulder. "I can't help but respond," she whispered, planting kisses along the smooth skin of his throat down to where the dark hairs curled in profusion over his chest. "You make me want. You make me ache."

"Your heart beats so hard. Do you want me that much?"

"Yes. Oh, yes!"

He pushed her onto the wide mattress and lay beside her, one leg nestled intimately between hers. New fires started low in her abdomen, burning to the core of her.

"I ache, too," he confessed, again with a rueful tone as if he laughed at himself and at this passion neither could deny. He slanted his mouth across hers and kissed her for a long time.

When he lifted his head and broke the kiss, she breathed deeply, inhaling his scent along with the air her whirling brain needed. "Kiss me again," she demanded.

"Glutton," he teased in the warmest tone imaginable. But he did as she requested.

His hands roamed her body, pausing at one breast, then the other, stroking until she writhed helplessly against his touch.

"I need you," she whimpered, clasping his face between her hands and giving him a thousand kisses.

"Such sweet passion," he whispered. "I never thought there would be anything like this for me."

She heard the loneliness in him. It touched her heart. He'd spent a lonely childhood just as she had. In many ways they were alike, she realized.

"Come to me," she invited. Leaning on an elbow, she pressed him onto the sheet and ravaged him as he'd done to her, stroking his lean body from neck to knee, stopping on the return trip to run her fingers through the dark patch of hair.

She smiled at his gasp when she ventured close to the rigid phallus. When she clasped him and stroked up and down, she heard his breath catch and hold for several heartbeats before he released it in a heavy sigh.

All thoughts fled her mind as they kissed again and again. His hands rubbed over her in a thousand caresses. She did the same to him. Soon there was no part of her unknown to his touch, nor any part of him a secret to her.

His fingers moved rhythmically in the moist womanly places of her body. Just when she thought she would come apart if he didn't come to her, he shifted them so that he rested between her thighs. She felt the probing touch and opened to him, ready to take him deep inside.

"Not yet, darling," he whispered. "First..."

She opened her eyes and watched him remove a packet from the table drawer. An image danced through her head—one of her and him and a laughing baby held between them. She ruthlessly erased the homey scene. It would never happen....

Jon suppressed the tremor that raced through him as he slipped back between the smooth thighs that opened to welcome him. He positioned himself carefully and began the journey into paradise, his control at full brake. He was close to climaxing, but he wouldn't go over the edge without her.

She was the most wonderful lover he'd ever known, as intent on giving pleasure as receiving it. He felt the same. With this woman, he didn't merely want to give her ecstasy in order to get his own. It was more than that.

He wanted her to know the wonder, to feel the bliss, just as he did. That need drove him before all others.

"Anne," he said, needing to say her name. "Easy, love. I don't want it to be over too soon."

"I've never wanted anyone like this." Her hands roamed over him in restless entreaty. When she gripped his hips and pulled him deep into her, as deep as they could go, he nearly came apart. He clenched his teeth and held on.

Pride filled him, that he could make his woman feel like this, that he could give her this....

He moved in her, loving the moist warmth of her desire that surrounded him. Gently, then harder as she indicated the need, he stroked the swollen bud of her pleasure until she rose to every thrust of his, her sweet entreaties filling his ears.

When she stiffened and held her breath, he continued stroking until she bucked urgently against him, sending him over the edge even as he fought to hold back. It was impossible.

Her whimpers of delight fed his own fulfillment. Her body contracted around his, holding him tightly, deeply within her until the energy totally drained from him.

"I love you," he said, the words welling up from the heart, sounding wise and beautiful and very, very right. "I love you." He sank into her, taking as much weight as possible on his arms to spare her.

She was having none of that. Instead, she pulled him tightly to her and kissed him along his throat, nipping at him like a playful terrier. "Stay," she whispered when he would have moved.

"I'm too heavy."

"Stay."

He sighed and let her take a bit more of his weight. The heated scent of their bodies was as potent as medicine. Strength flowed into him. With an arm around her, he turned them to the side, placing her leg over his hip so they could remain together.

An eternity of contentment went by.

Sometime later, Anne realized the steady pound she heard was the rain hitting the house. She rolled to her side and snuggled under the sheet, her back to Jon's chest.

"It's raining," he said, laying an arm over her waist.

"I like it. It adds a romantic touch...." Her tummy growled at that moment.

He chuckled. "We haven't had dinner. I'd better feed the beast. Which reminds me—I have to feed a couple of cows this evening, too." He stroked her abdomen, then lower, inciting little riots of sensation along her nerves.

"Jon," she said on a sighing breath.

"That was good, wasn't it?"

His breath fanned across her ear; then she felt his kiss on her temple as he rose to one arm and gazed out the window at the night sky. A light in the nearest greenhouse formed a backdrop so they could see the heavy fall of raindrops.

"Yes," she replied truthfully. "It was very good."

He kissed her neck, causing chills to dance along her spine. She clasped her thighs together, trapping his playful hand and stopping the light caresses.

"Stay in bed," he murmured, turning her and kissing her breasts until she lost her breath completely. "I'll call you when dinner is ready."

After pulling on his jeans, he left a terry robe and heavy tube socks at the end of the bed and headed for the kitchen. As soon as he'd left, she dashed into the bathroom to freshen up, put on the robe and socks, then raced down the stairs.

Jon was in the mudroom, putting on a yellow slicker like the ones she'd seen in cowboy movies.

"I want to go with you," she told him. That earned her a kiss, then he sorted through a box of rain gear and gave her a pair of boots and a slicker. When she was ready, he took her hand and led the way outside. They ran the short distance down the road to the barn.

Inside, he pulled to a stop outside a box stall. Anne rose to her tiptoes and peered over the top. Inside, snuggled in the straw was a cow and a very wobbly-legged calf.

"Ah, she's had it," Jon murmured. He perused the newborn. "A bull calf." He dipped a bucket in a feed sack and put it in the stall.

While he drew a fresh bucket of water, Anne stayed with the new mother and baby. The calf sucked her fingers when she tried to stroke its nose. She laughed shakily as a giant fist contracted inside her. She pulled her hand away.

The calf rooted its head under the cow's belly and found a teat. It suckled noisily.

Jon fed and watered some older calves in another pen, then returned and set the bucket in the corner of the stall. The cow drank, too. For the next few minutes, that was the only sound in the dim barn. Outside, the rain fell steadily, but inside, it was cozy and warm and deeply intimate.

Anne looked at Jon. He took his gaze off the calf and turned toward her. His eyes looked as dark as midnight and as deep as eternity. She was being drawn inside....

She blinked and looked away.

"Anne," he said.

"Is this all you need to do?" she quickly broke in.

He studied her for a second, then nodded. "Let's go back to the house. It's time we had our dinner."

Again he took her hand. They covered the distance from the barn to the house quickly. Anne joined him in the old-fashioned kitchen at the back of the house after they'd removed their boots and slickers.

He lifted her to the counter. "I was your first lover," he murmured. "We could have taken it more slowly."

"I was afraid you'd stop."

"I couldn't," he admitted. "Not unless you told me to." He gazed into her eyes. "You know I'll stop if you say so, don't you?" It was a vow.

Her throat constricted and she could only nod. He dropped a kiss on her forehead and began work on their belated dinner.

He heated an indoor grill and removed the steaks from a pan of wine marinade. After they were cooking and potatoes baking, he set the table and placed salads, already made, at each setting.

"Such efficiency. I'm impressed." She gave him an approving grin when he paused.

"Good husband material?" he inquired with a smile so tender it sent her heart into a spin and confused her at the same time.

"Sure. I'll write you a recommendation when you get ready to take the plunge."

"Thanks." The smile that hovered at the corners of his mouth touched her in ways she couldn't name.

She watched him grill the steaks and toast slices of French bread, but her thoughts focused on the future...a future when he would marry someone and have children. She wanted to ask if he planned to live here, in this house, but the question clogged in her throat and wouldn't come out.

It wasn't any business of hers. For now, she lived for the moment. She wouldn't think beyond that.

When he finished the kitchen chores, he carried her to the table, swinging her into his arms as easily as a crate of plants.

"You don't have to carry me," she protested.

"Yeah, you're so heavy, I might spring my back." He gave her an amused glance and placed her in a chair.

Going to a corner cupboard, he removed stemmed glasses and poured them each a glass of rich, red table wine. He took his place opposite her and handed her a glass.

"To us," he said with a smile she didn't quite understand. "And to a long and delightful affair."

Her heart dipped at the word. An affair was all she wanted. Of course it was. It was just that the word signaled the end before they'd hardly gotten started.

She smiled gamely and held up her glass. "To us." She sipped the wine.

Laughing, he picked up his fork and began eating, his gaze never leaving her. She had no doubts about his attraction to her. His attention made her feel beautiful and feminine.

During the meal, he charmed her with his humor and regaled her with tales of his boyhood. He'd loved adventure and had gotten into trouble because of it, which made it clear why he got along so well with the Ralston boys.

"No wonder the boys like you so much," she murmured at one point. "They recognize a kindred soul."

His smile faded into an expression she couldn't describe. Wistful, maybe. "Do you?" he challenged. The seriousness of the question alarmed her.

"Of course." She hit upon a safe topic. "Ellen and I hit it off from the moment she returned here to live. We've been friends since."

He gazed into her eyes and refused to let her look away. She drank from the wineglass and tried to still the tremor that invaded her hands.

"Yes, sometimes it's like that...from the first moment."

She knew he referred to them. She laughed, a nervous twitter that sounded fake to her ears. "The kiss..."

"Yes." His mouthed curved into a nostalgic smile that upended her heart and sent it tumbling down to her toes. "I wanted to kiss you from the moment I saw you. I didn't know why. But I knew I had to. Now..."

Again she had an impression of great tenderness flowing from him to her, engulfing her in dreams she'd learned, years ago, to live without. Her alarm increased. Definitely a lightening of mood was called for.

She laid down her utensils and glanced at the clock. "That was a wonderful meal. Do you realize it's almost midnight? I really should be getting home." She laughed and shook her head as if they were wayward children out on a lark.

Flames leapt into his eyes as he looked her over in a possessive manner. "I'm not going to let you go."

"Oh, dear, am I going to have to yell for help?"

Pushing his chair back, he rose and came to her. "Do you want to?" He lifted her from the chair and clasped her to his chest while he nuzzled along her temple.

"I . . . no," she admitted, unable to lie.

"Good." He carried her back to bed and placed her there as if she were one of the famous Fabergé jeweled eggs.

After removing the heavy socks, he untied the robe and pushed it open. Then he simply gazed at her, bringing a flush to her skin at his ardent appraisal.

"Beautiful," he murmured. "How did I ever get so lucky?"

Self-conscious under his scrutiny, she sat up and tossed the robe aside, then tugged at the snap on his jeans. He let her unzip them and push them over his hips; then he sat beside her and kicked them off.

She pulled him to her as she snuggled into the sheet and pulled the covers over them. He straightened so that he lay between her thighs, his body fitted over hers, warming her through and through.

The heat built in her. "I want you," she whispered, restless with the need for him that rose once more in her, stronger than before.

It was dangerous, the way he made her feel. The wild response he coaxed from her willing body came from deep inside and was more than physical. A flurry of panic froze her into stillness for a moment.

"What is it?" He kissed her down her throat, then lifted his head to look into her eyes.

"Nothing."

He touched her mouth with fingers that trembled slightly, as hers had earlier. "This *nothing* is pretty powerful. It makes us both shake like wet dogs on a cold night."

Again his tenderness was evident in his eyes. It melted right down inside her, turning her fear into a mist that burned away under the heat of his caress. She pulled him close, driven by an urgent sense of time's passage.

"Don't talk," she begged, kissing him madly, loving the hard planes of his bone structure under the taut flesh of his face, loving the abrasive glide of his body against hers, loving the miracle of him, of her... of man and woman.

They made love and slept, then woke at dawn.

"A new day," he murmured, his body cupped around hers as if they'd slept that way often.

"Everything is new." She twisted around to face him. "I never knew the human body had so much potential." She smiled at the inadequacy of the word. "There was so much pleasure."

"That's just the beginning," he promised on a husky note. "We'll just keep on getting better and better."

She laughed. "I can see us as a little old grandma and grandpa, still making love—" She stopped abruptly when she realized where her foolish tongue was taking her.

"So can I," he said in lazy amusement, obviously not catching her gaffe. He smoothed her tangled hair as he watched the sun rise above the horizon, bathing the remnant of storm clouds in pink and silver.

She breathed easy once more. She had to quit thinking about a future for them. That was definitely out.

The rumble of his stomach provided an excuse to break the intimate moment. "Are you as good at breakfast as you were at dinner?" She tweaked the hair near his nipple playfully.

He pressed her hand to the spot and held it there. His heart beat with steady rhythm against her palm. During their lovemaking, it had pounded in fierce excitement against her.

A teasing light sprang into his eyes. "I'll let you be the judge," he promised as he bent to kiss her breasts with sensuous familiarity. His hand roamed over her with equal ease.

She pretended to be indignant and pushed him away. "I meant at cooking. I'm starved."

He laughed with a carefree abandon she'd never heard from him. He sounded happy. It gave her such a strange feeling. . . .

"I'm not sure I can walk," he complained. "That was some workout. You may have to do the honors this morning."

She stretched and yawned, then swung her legs out of bed. The house was cold. She pulled on the socks and robe, then padded down the stairs and into the kitchen.

After starting the coffee, she headed back upstairs. The shower came on when she entered the bedroom. She stood in the middle of the room, unable to make up her mind about joining him. She wanted to, but was it wise?

"Coming?" he called out.

Forgetting wisdom, she flung off the clothing, shivered as the cool air hit her skin, then dashed for the shower.

Jon had his hands all soaped up and ready when she entered. He washed her with delicate attention to every part of her body, which set his libido to humming with the sexual tension generated just by being near her. He was soon near the exploding point.

"Are you sore?" he asked, seeing her wince as he rubbed her in an intimate spot.

"A little. It doesn't matter."

He held the detachable hose so he could rinse the soap away, then kissed the wet curls and buried his face against her. He teased her with his tongue, loving the warm taste of her, then he forced himself to finish the self-appointed task—torture, he corrected—of bathing her. He saw her gaze travel down his body and pause at the arousal he couldn't hide.

"Nothing to fear," he murmured, rising after rinsing her legs and feet. "Just a little morning exercise."

"Oh, yes, I see," she quipped with a bright, innocent smile. "Sit-ups." She stepped out of the shower.

He laughed so hard, his ribs hurt. By the time he followed her into the other room, she had dried off and was dressing. He slipped into fresh clothing as fast as he could and dashed down the stairs after her when she left the bedroom.

Entering the kitchen, he found she'd poured them each a cup of coffee and was now breaking eggs into a bowl. Milk and grated cheese stood ready on the counter.

"Omelet okay?" she asked.

"Anything." He devoured her with his eyes, wanting nothing more than to go back to bed and spend the day there, making love every hour on the hour. "I wish I weren't such a considerate lover," he complained, giving her a look of longing.

A hint of pink flushed her cheeks. She gave him a behave-yourself frown. He smiled, happier than he could ever remember being before in his life.

Love. That was the reason.

A sigh of contentment oozed out of him. God, but he felt like the king of the mountain this morning.

He watched as she brought their plates to the table, then returned behind the counter to butter the toast.

Because of her, he thought. All the happiness, the bubbling-with-life feelings, they were because of her. He needed to tell her, to talk about their future now that things were settled between them.

"Eat," she commanded.

"Bossy," he commented, giving her a mock frown. She could boss him to hell and back. He didn't care.

"Absolutely. Haven't you noticed?" She topped off their coffee mugs and took her place at the table.

"Yeah, maybe I have."

She peered at him suspiciously. "You're in a strange mood this morning."

"After a night of the best sex I ever had, I could probably leap tall buildings in a single bound."

Her glance was amused. "You would probably fall on your face and embarrass yourself."

"I love a practical woman." He leaned over the table and kissed her in spite of her mumbled protests and full mouth. "How soon can we be married?"

The smile left her. A premonition that he'd read the signs all wrong hit him. He returned her startled gaze with a steady one and kept the smile on his face.

"Who said anything about marriage?" she asked, her tone slipping from the amused to the decidedly cool register. She laid her fork down as if finished.

"I did." He pushed the dishes aside and folded his arms on the table. "Last night..." He shook his head slightly, trying to remember all they'd said in the heat of passion. "I told you last night that I loved you—"

She spun from the chair, acting like a frightened doe ready to run from a predator. "That was passion talking."

"That was me."

Anne heard the resolute belief in his voice, saw it in his eyes. "Falling in love... that isn't part of the game," she protested, feeling betrayed.

"Game? We've gone far beyond games." He stood and came to her, hovering over her, puzzlement and the beginnings of anger in his expression.

"It isn't fair. It's against the rules—"

He caught her shoulders. "What are you talking about? What we shared last night wasn't a pretense. It was real." He folded her against him. "Very real," he assured her and kissed the corner of her mouth.

"You might feel that way now, but what about later?"

"What are you talking about?"

"You're a man used to going your own way. You'll soon be restless again and want to move on. A wife is a hindrance to that type of life."

He relaxed and smiled. "I'm going to stay. When I first returned, I was planning to sell out and move on, but I put it off, telling myself I'd get more money if I fixed the place up a bit. I discovered I liked working on the old homestead. Then I met you, and I fell in love. I'm staying, Anne. Here's where we'll live and raise our family—"

She pulled out of his arms. "I don't want you to fall in love with me. I told you straight out that I wouldn't marry you. You're not the one—"

Catching her chin, he turned her face to his. "Right. You want an older man like your senator. Then why the hell didn't you spend last night in his bed instead of mine?"

She stared into his eyes for a long minute before she had to look away. "I wanted you," she explained. "It was passion. That's all it was between us."

"That's all you'll accept," he said slowly.

"Yes."

He released her and stepped back. She grabbed the back of the chair. Her legs had gone weak and shaky. She glanced at Jon, then away, unable to face the bleakness that had replaced the happiness in his eyes.

"I'm the wrong one," she whispered in a choked voice. "I'm not the one for you. You're not for me."

"You've decided?" he asked, his voice so quiet, it was like a death knell. "And that's that? No matter what I say?"

She wavered for a moment, wanting his love more than anything. But she couldn't give him the home and family he would want and had every right to expect. She couldn't.

"Yes, I've decided." Not looking at him, she walked out of the bright, friendly room, picked up her purse and headed for her car. The trip to town took forever.

9

<hr>

Anne ignored the telephone. Its shrill ring stopped before the answering machine came on. Her aunt had called several times that week. So had Jon. She didn't want to talk to anyone, especially Jon, who had broken the rules of an affair with his declaration of love and expectation of marriage.

It wasn't fair. She wanted an affair to remember all her life. One night wasn't enough for a lifetime of memories.

Her hands clenched on the coffee cup when the phone started ringing again. She dreaded going to the shop that morning. Her Christmas poinsettia order was due. Maybe Jon would send Pedro alone to delivery the pots of flowers.

No, he wouldn't. He was too stubborn for that.

She gritted her teeth until the racket stopped on the fourth ring. Leaping to her feet, she rinsed her cup, grabbed her purse and headed for the flower shop. There was work to be done.

Lina was in before her, bustling around the back room and making up corsages and boutonnieres for a ceremonial dinner at the country club that night. The younger woman was humming.

"Good morning. You sound happy." Anne tucked her purse up on a shelf and slipped an apron over her slacks and top.

Lina returned the greeting solemnly, then broke into a wide grin that startled Anne.

"What's happened?" Anne demanded, sensing what was coming.

Lina held her hand out. She wore a gold ring with a small diamond mounted on it.

Anne admired the stone and congratulated her employee. "It is from Steve, isn't it? You aren't eloping with a traveling salesman or something, are you?" she teased.

Lina laughed with delight. "I'm not eloping, and yes, it's from Steve. Who else could it be? My brothers would have a conniption if I let him get away. They've decided he's just the man for me." She rolled her eyes heavenward.

"Have you set a date?"

"The first Sunday in January. Will you...would you mind being my maid of honor?"

Anne couldn't refuse the shy entreaty in Lina's eyes, which were as dark and beautiful as ripe plums. "I'd be delighted." She picked up a pencil and pad. "What colors are you going to use? I'll provide the flowers."

"Oh, no, that's too much!"

"Nonsense. It isn't every day a girl gets married. Do you want one type of flower or a mixed bouquet?"

Anne helped Lina plan the details of the wedding while they completed the order for the country club dinner. When they were finished, Anne delivered them herself. She needed to get out of the shop and away from Lina's bubbling happiness for a while.

It wasn't that she begrudged her friend's engagement, but sometimes it was difficult to maintain the pretense that it wasn't something she wanted for herself.

She did, but it was out of the question. Since meeting Jon, she'd thought constantly of a future with him.

There, she'd admitted it. Now maybe she could forget and get on with her life, which had been very nice until two weeks and six days ago.

The kiss. That's what had started this whole impossible situation, this foolish dreaming. . . .

It didn't have to be a dream. She could reach out and take all she wanted. But would that be fair to Jon? He was good with children and would make an excellent father. Given her family medical history, she was afraid to chance having a child.

Frowning, she stacked the last container of boutonnieres in the refrigerator at the club, collected her check from the office and drove back to town. After parking the delivery van, she paused before going into the shop. She felt so restless.

Ellen yoo-hooed and pointed to the diner. Anne walked up the street and met her friend at the door. They went inside and ordered coffee and muffins.

Ellen opened the conversation. "Lina showed me her ring."

"It was lovely, wasn't it?" Anne said, forcing enthusiasm into her voice and smile.

"So when are you and Jon going to set a date?"

Anne's smile faded a little. "Never."

"That's not what I hear."

Startled, Anne surveyed her friend. "What do you hear?" she asked cautiously, trying not to act the least interested.

"Jon Sinclair was looking at engagement rings this morning."

"He what?"

"He was over at Main Street Jewelry looking at that big diamond displayed in the window."

Anne's heart did a tap dance on her breastbone. He couldn't be planning to give it to her, not after she'd refused him last weekend. "He wouldn't dare," she said aloud.

"He looked pretty serious," Ellen said and gave her a squinty-eyed scrutiny. "You stayed with him last Saturday night. That might have led him to believe you want more than a one-night stand, don't you think?"

"How did you know that?"

Ellen shrugged. "I suspect everyone in town knows it. What does the gorgon say?"

"Aunt Marge has had a migraine this week. She's only called four times to warn me about hormones and the mistakes *those* can lead to." Anne put a hand to her forehead and groaned. "I think I could learn to hate small towns."

"Now, now." Ellen patted her hand. "Here comes Jon."

Anne jerked around. Sure enough, Jon was stalking up the street. He looked grim as death. He walked into the diner and threw a leg over the chair back and joined them.

"I'll leave," Ellen said and did so before Anne could do more than splutter a protest.

Jon gave her a nasty smile. "Alone at last."

Refusing to acknowledge the tremors inside, she lifted her chin and assumed a nonchalant air. "This is a private party. Did you get an invitation?"

He ignored her. "You've ruined my sterling reputation," he announced. "What are you going to do about it?"

"Nothing," she said.

"I figured that would be your attitude. I'm giving you one last chance. Marry me or face the consequences."

For a moment, she thought of how easy it would be to say yes, to no longer fight her feelings and his. The word trembled on her tongue, ready to drop like a golden pearl into the tense silence. She closed her eyes and thought of the family they could never have. Praying for strength, she faced him.

"I told you I wouldn't marry you. I explained all that days ago." She gave him a frown that didn't quell him in the least.

"Yeah, the older man and all. Tell me again. I still don't get it, especially when you go to pieces in *my* arms."

"Shh," she hissed, looking around to see if any of the other four patrons heard his accusation. It was so unfair of him to bring that night—that wonderful, never-to-be-forgotten night— into the quarrel.

He shook his head sadly. "I'd hoped you'd listen to reason. There's a ring over at the jeweler's that's pretty nice. If you'd be reasonable and take it—" He trailed off and stared a challenge at her.

If he only knew how very reasonable she was trying to be for his sake. She had to end this before she flung herself into his arms and grabbed everything he offered. Anger was her only defense. "*Me* be reasonable? Who keeps insisting on marriage when I told you straight off that I would *not* marry you?"

The room stilled to absolute silence. She realized she'd been practically shouting.

"I do," he said, sounding perfectly logical about answering her rhetorical question. "I want marriage. That's the only way you'll repair my reputation."

"Too bad. I guess you'll have to sue me for defamation of character." She tried a cynical smile and managed to hold it on her mouth by force of will.

He sighed. "Well, there's no help for it, then. I'll have to go to plan two." He took a drink of her coffee, grimaced at the sweetness, then rose. He looked down at her with a strange smile, sort of tender, sort of amused. "The poinsettias are in. Pedro and Steve are unloading them now. I'll help them finish. See you tonight." He went to the door. "At six."

"No, don't. Leave me alone. I'm very busy, Christmas and all. My father is due home any day now," she warned, not above using any resource at hand to deflect his pursuit.

He gave her a pitying smile. "Plan two is going to be rough." He ambled out.

Stunned, Anne sat without moving for a moment, trying to figure out what he was going to do and what she should do to defuse whatever he had in mind.

A few titters of laughter flew around her head. Heat rose to her face, and she fled the diner for the relative peace of the flower shop. There she hid in the back room, making up bouquets, while Lina took care of the customers. She felt like a refugee.

The rest of the day she kept glancing out the windows of the shop, not sure what she was expecting, but fearing the worst.

After all, men were mule-headed creatures. Jon wasn't about to take rejection gracefully. There was only one thing to do— she'd have to be more stubborn than he was.

She and Lina arranged a poinsettia display on tiered shelves in front of the windows before closing.

Five o'clock came and went without incident.

The streets were crowded on Friday when she finally left the shop. People stayed in town on Friday night to cash their paychecks, shop and take in a movie or have a meal at one of the local restaurants. She breathed a sigh of relief when she made it to her house without incident.

Home, safe and sound.

Her peace didn't last long. A truck, actually a rival florist van, stopped on the street in front of her house. The driver got out and brought a bouquet of red roses to her door. He studied the note in his hand, set the vase on the porch and left without giving her a chance to refuse the gift.

"Oh," she fumed. She grabbed the telephone and punched out Jon's number.

He answered on the first ring. "Sinclair."

"Listen, you—"

"Right on time," he commented. "Did you like the roses?"

"Don't send me any more flowers."

"I won't. I'll bring them myself. I assume you know the language of flowers." He hung up.

She banged the receiver down, but that didn't still the agitation in her breast. She was primed to fight, but Jon wasn't cooperating. She felt like going to his place and socking him when he opened the door.

Except if she went out there, she might not get back before dawn. She clenched her hands against the hunger that urged her to accept all she could get from him.

She had to be fair, she reminded herself, and subdued the willful longing. She brought the flowers in and plunked them on the coffee table. Their scent filled the air.

The night was long, dark and sleepless. At six, she rose, dressed, put on a pot of coffee and went to the porch to retrieve the paper.

She stared in helpless surprise. Pots of forget-me-nots lined the sidewalk from the porch to the street. They were covered in buds ready to burst into bloom at the first touch of the sun.

She pressed a hand to her throat. In the language of flowers, forget-me-nots meant faithfulness. In chivalrous times, they'd meant the lover would forever be faithful to his love.

"I'll throw cocklebur seeds in his fields," she threatened aloud. She grabbed the paper and dashed back inside. She didn't want to see any of her neighbors' knowing smiles.

She returned to the kitchen and ate a quick breakfast of cereal and toast, then grimly read the day's news.

At nine, she left to go to work. She saw curtains shift as she walked down the flower-strewn path to the street. She thrust her chin into the air. She would not be coerced by Jon's brand of foolishness. He'd soon tire of his game.

At noon, the plants had been changed to wallflowers. *Love in spite of adversity.* If a knight sent those to his lady, it meant he would love her no matter what the opposition, whether it came from her, her father or the king. Love would persevere.

Honestly!

When she left the house after eating a meager peanut butter-and-jelly sandwich, the flowers had changed again.

"Primroses," she muttered and stopped in the middle of the sidewalk, trying to recall what they meant. "Youth," she finally recalled and looked at the blooms, puzzled by the message.

She spied a note attached to one flower stem. Plucking it from the plant, she read the message. "Gather ye rose-buds while ye may / Old time is still a-flying / And the same sweet flower that blooms today / Tomorrow may be a-dying."

"Twenty-five is not old," she protested with a glare down the road toward his ranch. "I've plenty of time to...to marry and..." She thought of the future she'd never have.

Loneliness drifted over her as she walked slowly to the shop. Jon would get over her. He'd find someone else to marry and share the good life. They'd have children, perfect children.

Lina gave her a secretive smile when she tossed her purse on a shelf and got back to work. Anne paused. Was the whole town in on Jon's practical jokes?

"We have several rush orders to fill," the younger woman said. "They're too complicated for me. If you'll make them up, I'll deliver them."

Anne looked over the requests. The country club wanted fresh bouquets for Sunday. Nothing unusual in that. She picked up the next order. It was for her. From Jon.

He wanted an arrangement of pansies and rosemary. Pansies, thoughtfulness. Rosemary, remembrance. *I think of you all the time. I will remember you forever.*

She ignored the order and worked on the country club's request. At four, Lina left for the day, the back of her compact pickup filled with baskets of flowers. Anne straightened the shop, vacuumed the floor and shined the glass countertops. All was in order for Monday.

Walking home, she admitted she'd be glad when her father arrived. She no longer wanted to be alone. They could do their Christmas shopping together. She'd hardly bought a gift yet and time was growing short. The line about gathering rosebuds came back to haunt her. She had plenty of time.

She kept a wary eye on her house as she approached, not sure what to expect. An herb pot, three feet tall, sat on the porch. Rosemary grew from the side openings while pansies filled the top space. Unexpected tears filled her eyes. Darn Jon Sinclair!

Forcing the emotions at bay, she went inside. "Dad?" she called, seeing the lights on.

He came out of the spare bedroom, a smile on his face, his arms open. She leapt into them and held on as if he were the one rock that would anchor her securely to common sense.

They talked until midnight. Setting down his hot chocolate cup, he mentioned casually, "A letter from Marge was waiting for me when I returned from Europe. She seems to be worried about you and some young man she suspects of having vile designs on your virtue. Do I need to punch someone out, or should I tell Marge to mind her own business?"

Her father had come to her rescue in the past when she and Aunt Marge hadn't seen eye to eye, but there was nothing he could do in this case. She clung to her resolve not to see Jon again. "There's nothing to tell. I—it's over."

Her father studied her for a long minute. His eyes looked sad. "I was never here for you when you were growing up. Why would you confide in me now?" The question was rhetorical.

"It isn't that," she began, but couldn't lie. Instead, she asked, "Why didn't you ever come home?"

"I couldn't," he said. "When your mother died, it was like the world ended. I couldn't stand to return. I took you with me until I realized you needed a home and a place to grow up. When you were three, I listened to Marge and let you live with them. I came home when telephones calls weren't enough. Sometimes I had to see you, to hold you. I was afraid you'd forget me."

"Never," she murmured, filled with compassion.

"When you were older, you seemed happy and settled here. I realized you didn't need me barging in your life. Marge said you were always upset for weeks after I left."

"I was. I missed you and I'd mope some. Aunt Marge worried about me, afraid I'd die if I got the slightest sniffle. I think she was afraid for me to travel with you."

He nodded. "I want you to be happy, baby. If there's something I can do to help with Sinclair—"

"No, there isn't," she said quickly. "He'll go away soon. And then everything will go back to the way it used to be."

"Will it?" her father questioned with a wise smile.

At nine, Anne woke with a start, feeling she'd overslept and missed something important. Refusing to let herself rush, she rose, washed up and dressed. She went to the kitchen and put on a pot of coffee... then she ran to the front porch.

Nothing. Not a flower in sight.

The disappointment was so acute, she felt like crying. Regaining her dignity, she picked up the heavy weekend paper, glanced at the sky where a helicopter beat a throbbing crescendo against the Sunday-morning quiet and returned to the kitchen. She'd barely gotten seated when the telephone rang.

She stared at it, afraid to answer, afraid not to. Finally she picked it up. "Hello?" Her voice squeaked, and she sounded as breathless as a teenager.

"Anne, turn on the morning news, Channel 5. Hurry!" Ellen said, laughter permeating her words. She hung up.

Mystified, Anne hurried into the living room and turned on the television set. Apprehension swamped her as she waited for the screen to lighten and show the picture. The announcer's voice droned at her.

"Romance is alive and well in one part of the state. One suitor decided to say it with flowers in a big way. Here's our on-the-scene reporter."

Over the noise of helicopter rotors, another reporter told of a case of "true love" in the Texas delta country.

Anne didn't hear a word the man said after that. She stared in shocked disbelief at the television.

There...there on the front lawn of the courthouse of *her town*, as viewed from the air, was a huge red heart made of flowers. Inside the heart, in tall letters formed by white mums, was inscribed Jon Loves Anne. An arrow of golden mums pierced the heart.

"Is that for you?" her father asked, coming into the living room. He smelled of a fresh shower and shave. "Jon Sinclair loves Anne Hyden—is that the message?"

"Yes," she whispered. "Oh," she cried, whirling around. "I'll send him a bouquet of poison ivy. I'll boil him in oil of roses. I'll... I'll..." She burst into tears.

Perplexed, her father handed her a handkerchief and held her as if she were still four and her favorite doll had been eaten by a neighbor's dog.

Jon gave the poster board sign a critical once-over. He deepened the color in the last letters of the message, then wondered what he would do next if this didn't work.

He'd expected to hear from Anne that morning, either by telephone or in person. She'd neither called nor shown up at his ranch. Neither had she turned out to see his handiwork on the courthouse lawn.

She was the hardest nut to crack he'd ever come across. But she loved him. She had to. Nothing else would explain why she'd let him make love to her, why she came apart each time they touched.

He felt the same. It was just a matter of showing her that they were meant for each other. But he couldn't figure out why she was fighting their inevitable fate so hard.

Ellen hadn't a clue, either.

It was maddening. He wanted to go over to Anne's house and confront her, but he'd decided a lighter touch was needed. He'd court her with humor and patience.

Patience. He cursed a solid round of all the bad words he'd ever heard. Patience? When it was all he could do not to tear over there and make love to her until she agreed to marry him and live with him forever...

He couldn't do that. It would only make her that much more stubborn. She was a strong-willed woman. He wouldn't have her any other way. Just thinking about all the arguments and making up they'd do throughout their lives quickened his blood.

A grim smile flitted over his face and was gone. Things were getting serious now. He'd have an affirmative answer soon or know the *real* reason why she refused him.

He waved the sign around until the marker ink dried. Glancing at his watch, he realized he had to leave. He gathered up the signs and headed for his truck. He'd timed this little surprise for when church let out. That's when the most people would be in town.

Saying a prayer for success, he gunned the engine and headed for his reluctant sweetheart's house. Nothing would keep him from her. It was merely a matter of how much convincing she would take.

Doubt swept over him. God, he'd never been so nervous.

*   *   *

Anne squinted against the bright sunlight when she stepped outside the brick church. After the service, her father had made plans with Aunt Marge, then lingered to speak to old friends.

The wait had given her time to check the moisture content of the floral arrangements on the altar table and to pluck off a fading bloom or two. Now she paused to let her eyes adjust to the brightness of the noon sun.

With an apprehensive frown, she looked toward the courthouse, not sure what to expect. The heart was still there for all the world to see. She set her lips together.

The story had been picked up by the wire services and all the major stations had shown the aerial view she'd seen earlier. A couple of reporters had nosed around, but no one had given them any information on the couple.

Thank goodness for that. She didn't think she could have borne being questioned about this harebrained idea. If she ever saw Jon Sinclair again, she was going to do something drastic.

What? a voice inside her inquired. Kiss him until he passed out in her arms?

Sighing, she joined her father. Her aunt and uncle insisted she and her father join them at the country club for lunch. She cried off going, saying she had some work to see to, but urged her father to go. She really preferred to be alone.

He looked her over with tender concern, then agreed to go with his in-laws and catch up on the community news. He patted Anne's shoulder and gave her an understanding smile before they left.

She waved them off and headed home.

Coward, she chided. She was going to hide in her house until this blew over or hell froze, whichever came first.

She reached her house without incident, but her sense of safety didn't last long. Another vase was waiting for her beside the door. It contained one red rose.

Behind her, she heard a door slam. Whirling, she witnessed Jon coming across the street. He carried a sign.

She stared, too stunned to breathe, much less move.

He began walking up and down in front of her house with his sign over his shoulder. The sign read Unfair To Fairy Godmothers.

She returned to the end of the sidewalk. "That doesn't make any sense," she informed him.

"Yes, it does." He gave her a slitted scrutiny. "Our fairy godmothers obviously worked hard to get us together. You're probably messing up some celestial plan that could affect mankind for centuries into the future."

"Ha."

"So skeptical. We'll have to work on that." He grinned at her, a slow grin that spread to his eyes as he looked her over.

Her heart melted. She pummeled it back into shape. "You and me—it isn't in the stars."

"Yes, it is. You just don't see it yet." He continued walking up and down the public sidewalk.

A car sped by and honked its horn. Jon waved to the laughing occupants, who were residents of the town and well-known to Anne. A wave of embarrassment rolled over her.

"I'm not standing out here and arguing with you about it. You can just make a fool of yourself alone," she informed him.

He shrugged and continued walking.

She went inside and changed clothes, sorry that she'd turned down Aunt Marge's offer. It would serve him right if he paraded up and down in front of an empty house all afternoon.

After hanging up her Sunday outfit, she crept into the living room and peered out the window. Pedro had joined Jon. His sign read Two Deductions Are Better Than One. The Ralston boys were there, too, flouting poster board advice. Kiss A Frog and Find A Prince were the sayings on their signs.

"Damnation," she muttered.

A car parked across the street next to the school yard. Ellen and Lina climbed out. "We brought lunch," Ellen called.

The boys ran to help carry the food. They traipsed up the walk. Jon and Steve joined them. Soon there was a picnic lunch taking place on Anne's front porch. She stalked to the open door and stuck her hands on her hips, trying to look tough while her heart attempted to club its way out of her chest.

"Come on," Ellen invited, waving a quarter section of broiled chicken at her. "Lunch is getting cold."

Anne opened the screen door and stepped outside. Jon moved over and made room for her on the steps. She gingerly sat beside him, wondering if she'd gone as crazy as he obviously had.

She nodded toward the signs propped against the porch railing. "Very original."

"I'd hoped you might like them." He tilted his head and studied her. "Although you appeared more angry than amused when I first arrived."

Ellen, Lina, Steve and the boys listened avidly to the conversation. Anne set her lips firmly together.

"The frog one was my idea," the older of the Ralston boys informed her proudly.

"He saw it on TV," the younger one claimed.

Anne glanced at them, then at Jon. "I feel like the latest episode of a soap opera." She managed a smile.

He chuckled. The sound dipped right down inside her and took up residence, vibrating in a low, caressing hum while she tried to ignore the sensation. If things could be different...

If fate had been kinder, she'd marry him in a flash, she admitted. The loneliness of the years ahead yawned before her. She knew she wouldn't marry Randall. It wouldn't be fair. He deserved someone who would love him with all her heart.

Hers was already taken.

She gave Jon a sideways glance and saw him studying her. His gaze was lambent with humor and tenderness. It made her ache. She looked away.

The boys filled most of the conversation until their dad stopped by and picked them up. "Nice flowers," the fire chief called before driving off.

Ellen and Lina exchanged a glance. Lina nudged Steve. "It's time we were going, too."

"Right, things to do and people to see," Ellen explained cheerfully. She gave Anne a meaningful look, then packed up their debris. The other three left.

Jon and she were alone.

"Why, Anne?" he asked quietly. He turned and probed deeply into her eyes, looking for answers.

She knew if she told him the truth, he'd insist on marrying her anyway. He'd say the lack of children didn't matter, but she thought it would. Maybe not now, but someday it might.

"Tell the truth and foil the devil," he suggested on a lighter note when she didn't reply.

"I told you my plans from the first. I like my life the way it is." She held his gaze as long as she could before she looked away. Lying to him was the hardest thing.

"I have a buyer for the ranch," he said out of the blue.

Her heart crunched into shards at the information she knew was coming. He was going to leave. It was better that way. It was. He'd forget. And she'd get on with her life.

"Tell me you don't love me," he insisted. "Tell me and I'll walk away and never bother you again."

She opened her mouth, but no words came forth. He'd given her an easy way out, but she couldn't say the hurtful things that would put an end to their involvement.

"Tell me," he said.

She shook her head.

"You do love me," he concluded, relief in his voice. "So why can't we marry as people usually do?"

"My mother died when I was born," she said.

Surprise flicked across his face at the strange turn of subject, but he nodded, indicating his willingness to listen.

"She had a congenital heart defect. I have it, too."

He waited a moment. "So? Ellen said yours wasn't dangerous, that you could live an ordinary life."

"No." She spread her hands in a hopeless manner. "I told you about going to my old college flame's home to meet his parents, remember?"

"Yes."

"That was when I realized...his mother was so snooty—asking me a thousand questions about my bloodlines as if I were a brood mare. It made me angry. I realized if I should die, I couldn't bear the thought that she might raise a child of mine and turn it into someone like her. Of course, I also realized my boyfriend brought me home to defy her. I wasn't a debutante or anything his mother would approve of.''

Jon snorted in disgust. ''Good thing you got rid of him.''

She hesitated. ''There's something else, something more serious than what might happen to me. Any child of mine would most likely be born with serious heart defects. It runs in my family,'' she quickly added when he gave her an impatient glance. ''I can't take that risk. I'd never do that to a child.''

He laid his hands on her shoulders. ''I'm not marrying you to have children. That would be a bonus, but it's one I can live without. I don't want to live without you.''

She shook her head. ''I can't. Please. Don't make this harder than it has to be. I'm trying to be fair—''

He let her go. When she risked a glance at him, she saw dejection. It was so at odds with his strength and determination, she almost wept. She stared off into the distance when he rose and stood looking down at her.

''I won't give up that easily. This is our future, and I think it could be something special. Think about it.'' He walked down the sidewalk. After tossing the signs in the back, he got in the truck and drove off.

She watched him go, pain eating a hole in her heart.

10

Anne stayed inside the house the rest of the afternoon. Hiding, she admitted. She didn't think she could take any more confrontations with Jon. Her resistance was rubbing away like limestone under running water.

Darn it, she was trying to be noble and all that. She didn't want to shackle him with a wife who might keel over dead at any moment. Not that she thought she would.

But still, she did have to take six penicillin tablets just to have her teeth cleaned. It was a fact that heart ailments ran in the family. If she married Jon, she'd want children. . . .

She heard a car pull into her drive. A door slammed a second later. She steeled herself for another battle.

"Anne?"

The visitor was Aunt Marge. Anne grimaced and considered not answering. Unfortunately, the door was open, indicating she was home. She laid aside the book she was reading and went to the door.

"Aunt Marge, come in," she invited cordially. "Where are Uncle Joe and Dad?"

"At the golf course," her aunt replied, entering and leading the way into the living room, her mouth pursed in disapproval.

Anne half smiled. Uncle Joe had played golf for forty years and lived with his wife's umbrage. Anne doubted things were going to change anytime soon.

Taking a chair, she folded her hands in her lap and waited to see what brought her aunt away from the Sunday-afternoon gossip session of the Richport Beautification Committee.

"Jon Sinclair was seen at the jewelry store a few minutes ago," she announced. "He apparently talked Daryl into opening so he could buy that ring on display in the window."

Anne clutched a hand to her chest. Her heart beat so hard, it ached. Or maybe the pain was caused by the strange piercing sensations that shot through her at odd intervals. A roaring wind in her ears drowned out other noises.

"Anne, Anne," Marge remonstrated sadly. "You can't be thinking of marriage, not to a man like him."

"Why not to a man like him?" Anne was offended for Jon's sake. He'd shown her only tenderness. He'd been concerned that their passion not frighten her or cause her discomfort in any way. He'd given her his love, asked her to be his wife. What more could a woman ask of a man?

She knew he wasn't the rambling man she'd first thought. She didn't think her father was, either. They'd just had nothing to tie their roots to. Now Jon did. Or he thought he did.

Marge frowned at her. "Your heart, of course. You mustn't get overexcited. You know you must be careful."

"I've been careful all my life," Anne said, old rebellion stirring. She yearned to be free of past constraints and to find a new life. If Jon wanted her as she was, then why couldn't they have a satisfying life? They could adopt children.

Hope sprang up like a tiny seedling. Perhaps there was a future for them. If she were brave enough to reach for it . . .

"And I'll see that she's careful the rest of her life," a male voice cut into the strained conversation.

Anne whirled around. Jon stood on the porch. Others stood behind him, but she couldn't see who they were. They came in.

"Jon. Uncle Joe. Dad." She couldn't figure out what was happening. The three men looked geared for battle.

Jon gave her a probing look as he crossed the room. He dropped to his haunches in front of her chair and pried her clasped hands apart in order to hold them in his own. "It'll be all right," he assured her. Surely a strange thing to say.

She stared at their entwined hands, aware of the warmth and gentleness in his touch. He kissed the back of her hand, leaving the sweet imprint of his lips to burn into her skin.

"Tell her," Jon said over his shoulder.

Her father and Uncle Joe entered the living room. Her dad sat in the other easy chair while Uncle Joe joined his wife on the sofa. A tremor ran through Anne. Jon squeezed her hands and let go. He sat on the arm of her chair and nodded.

Her father cleared his throat. "There seems to be some confusion about what you can or can't do," he said to Anne.

"Really, Loury," her aunt started.

Uncle Joe laid a hand on her arm. "Hush, Marge."

She gave him an indignant glare. He shook his head at her, a warning to keep silent. Marge snapped her lips together. Twin red spots burned in her cheeks.

Anne was amazed at this display. She turned back to her father. "Confusion about what? I don't know what you mean."

"Jon tells me you think you shouldn't have children."

She nodded slowly, wondering what he was getting out.

"Doc's been taking care of you since you were hardly more than a baby," he said gently. "Did he ever tell you not to have children?"

"She has a heart condition," Marge burst out. "Of course she can't have children. It's too dangerous."

"That's not true," her father said. "With antibiotics, the risk during pregnancy is no more than any normal expectant mother would experience."

Anne looked from her aunt to her father in confusion. "But my mother died, and she had the same thing I do."

Her dad shook his head sadly. "Your mother died of other complications—a broken heart perhaps and stubbornness."

"What?" Anne said, stunned.

"We'd quarreled about my business trips. She ignored the instructions she was given during pregnancy. She was anemic and run-down when her term ended. She didn't take her vitamins or her medication." He spread his hands in a helpless gesture. "I didn't realize it. I've blamed myself ever since. She caught a cold, then pneumonia. She was burning with fever when she went into premature labor. I came home from a short trip and rushed her to the hospital, but it was too late by then."

"You mean . . . it wasn't her heart?" Hope splintered in Anne, throwing shafts of brilliance through the doubts that had always shadowed her future.

"No. Mitral valve prolapse—it used to be called a heart murmur—is relatively common and no big problem with modern medicine and a few simple precautions."

"But..." Anne turned to her aunt. "You told me I had to be careful, that I couldn't risk having children."

Marge leapt to her feet. "My sister died in my arms. My babies lived only a few hours or days. I took you when you were hardly more than a toddler and raised you, loving you as if you were my own. When the doctor told me you, too, had a defect, I was terrified. I couldn't bear to lose you. You were all Joe and I had of the future."

"And now we can't rob Anne of hers," Uncle Joe put in softly. "I knew you were overzealous in Anne's care, but I didn't realize you'd frightened the child into thinking she couldn't marry and have a family."

The red spread over Marge's face. "I don't want her to die," she said. Her eyes shone with tears. Her voice shook. "She's all we have."

"We have each other." Uncle Joe stood and faced her. "I'll always regret the deaths of our boys, but my life has never felt empty. You've been a good wife and I've had many happy years as your husband. I hope these youngsters are as lucky as we've been in our love."

Anne and the other two men stayed silent, the moment between husband and wife a fragile one.

"Anne was a wonderful gift in our lives," Uncle Joe continued gently, "but now it's time to let her go. She has her own life to live. We can't tell her whom to love any more than we can tell the wind which way to blow. That's her decision."

The silence lengthened to unbearable limits after he quit speaking.

Marge drew a deep breath and looked from her husband to Anne. Her gaze lingered on her niece, then she turned to Jon. "Anne loves to walk in the rain. She forgets her jacket. You will take care of her, won't you?"

She sounded angry, but Anne recognized the emotional strain that thinned her aunt's voice into a querulous tone.

Jon must have, too. His expression softened, and he nodded gravely. "You have my word."

Tears blurred Anne's vision. She stood, took three steps across the carpet and threw her arms around her aunt. "You'll always be my favorite aunt," she whispered. "No matter what."

Marge patted her awkwardly. "I'm your only aunt," she said with a return of her acerbic tongue, pulling back and wiping her eyes with the handkerchief her husband handed over.

"And you'll be godmother to all my children," Anne promised, her own voice rather squeaky.

Uncle Joe beamed all around. "Shall we go to that gossip session known as the Richport Beautification Committee? I think we have some hot items to share. Loury, better join us. These young people need some time to sort themselves out."

"We have to put up the tree," Anne reminded her father. It was something she'd always saved, something for them to do together when he came home. Then she looked at Jon hesitantly.

"I'll help," he said in his quiet, woodsy voice that soothed and excited at the same time.

Anne looked at her father. He came to her and gave her a hug. "Be happy. I think I'll spend the night with Joe and Marge. We have a lot of old memories to share. Tomorrow we'll put up the tree."

A blush climbed her face as her father shook hands with her lover and they exchanged one of those solemn male looks.

"You're right about one thing," Marge said to her husband, pausing on the porch. "We've had a wonderful marriage."

Anne held her breath in amazement.

"We'll discuss this later," Uncle Joe suggested in a husky tone, guiding her down the steps.

"Maybe I should go down to the local pub and entertain myself for a couple of hours," Loury Hyden suggested.

"Oh, come on," Marge ordered. "We're not going to embarrass you by billing and cooing in your presence. People of *my* generation have a sense of propriety."

Anne sighed happily. Everything would be all right.

After they were gone, the song of a lazy cricket stirred the air briefly, then it, too, fell silent.

Anne looked at Jon. He watched her without speaking. She took a deep breath and waited. "Well?" she said at last.

He smiled slightly.

She wasn't sure what to do. When the silence grew too long, her uncertainty frayed into anger. Did he want her to make the first move? Should she declare her love? Fall at his feet?

She was willing to do any of the above.

Brushing a wisp of hair from her face, she opened her mouth, not sure what was going to come out. "Did you buy a ring this afternoon?"

"Yes."

He didn't offer more. The cad. Her confidence grew at the tenderness in his eyes which he couldn't hide. A smile pulled at her lips. "For me?"

He nodded.

She sighed dramatically. "Are you going to give it to me? Or do I have to find it myself?" She couldn't keep the smile in any longer. It bloomed full on her face.

"Are you going to marry me?"

"Yes."

"Soon?"

"Yes." She gave him an impatient frown. She wanted to be in his arms.

He stood and held his arms out, inviting him to search his lean, strong body. She went to him. Her wanton heart boomed with happiness. The tempest inside her built rapidly.

She ran her hands over his torso and down each leg, over his chest and down to his thighs. He caught his breath, then let it out in a heavy gush.

Leaning into him, she reached around and explored his back. There was a bulge in his hip pocket.

"Ah, a clue," she murmured. She eased the square box free, then held it between them.

He took it from her, opened it and removed the ring. He tossed the box into the chair. Lifting her hand, he held the ring at the tip of her ring finger. "Will you marry me, my sweet Anne?" he whispered.

She hesitated. The lessons of a lifetime were hard to overcome. "There's so much I want," she whispered. "Us. Our children."

"We'll have them," he promised. "First we'll have you checked over by the best heart specialist in the States. Then, God willing..." He waited, a world of patience in his stance. It was up to her.

"What if something happens? What if we have a child and..." She couldn't voice the rest.

"Life doesn't come with any guarantees. One minute it's mums blooming all around, the next it's an angry bull charging right at you." He smiled. "We'll take it however it comes. You and I. Together."

It was the promise of a lifetime. A woman would be stupid to give it up.

"Then, I would be honored," she said.

Happiness beamed across his face. He pushed the ring all the way down, then kissed her finger where it rested.

"Oh, before I forget." He removed a bill from his pocket and tucked it into her hand. "Let me know when I've used that up."

She got a glimpse of it before he kissed her. It was a five-thousand-dollar bill. An orange one.

"Play money?" she shrieked, drawing back and giving him a glare while holding the laughter in.

"Yeah." He nuzzled her ear, sending chills down her neck. "We're going to play house for a long time."

Sweeping her against him, he kissed her passionately, desperately, hungrily. Her heart skipped beats. She went dizzy. And breathless. And weak in the knees.

She didn't worry. She knew the symptoms now.

This was love.

* * * * *

Sneak Previews of January titles, from *Yours Truly*™:

JUST THE WAY YOU ARE
by Janice Kaiser

It all started with one little white lie to one very gorgeous man. But secretary Britt Kingsley had no idea she'd been fibbing to Mr. Right. And now she's in love—with a man who knows her as three different women!

THE WEDDING DATE
by Christie Ridgway

When Emma's ex-fiancé invites her to his wedding, she tells *everyone* about the new man she's bringing. But she doesn't even know any men! So she hires a date—for a week. But after all the wedding festivities, Emma wants him forever.

≈≈≈≈≈≈

Available this month, from *Yours Truly*™:

CHRISTMAS KISSES FOR A DOLLAR
by Laurie Paige

HOLIDAY HUSBAND
by Hayley Gardner

It's our 1000th Special Edition and we're celebrating!

Join us these coming months for some wonderful stories in a special celebration of our 1000th book with some of your favorite authors!

Diana Palmer
Debbie Macomber
Phyllis Halldorson

Nora Roberts
Christine Flynn
Lisa Jackson

Plus miniseries by:

Lindsay McKenna, Marie Ferrarella, Sherryl Woods and Gina Ferris Wilkins.

And many more books by special writers!

And as a special bonus, all Silhouette Special Edition titles published during Celebration 1000! will have **_double_** Pages & Privileges proofs of purchase!

Silhouette Special Edition...heartwarming stories packed with emotion, just for you! You'll fall in love with our next 1000 special stories!

Are your lips succulent, impetuous, delicious or racy?

Find out in a very special Valentine's Day promotion—THAT SPECIAL KISS!

Inside four special Harlequin and Silhouette February books are details for THAT SPECIAL KISS! explaining how you can have your lip prints read by a romance expert.

Look for details in the following series books, written by four of Harlequin and Silhouette readers' favorite authors:

Silhouette Intimate Moments #691
Mackenzie's Pleasure by *New York Times* bestselling author Linda Howard

Harlequin Romance #3395
Because of the Baby by Debbie Macomber

Silhouette Desire #979
Megan's Marriage by Annette Broadrick

Harlequin Presents #1793
The One and Only by Carole Mortimer

Fun, romance, four top-selling authors, plus a FREE gift! This is a very special Valentine's Day you won't want to miss! Only from Harlequin and Silhouette.

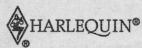

VAL96

INTRODUCING...

A collection of award-winning books by award-winning
authors! From Harlequin and Silhouette.

Falling Angel
by Anne Stuart

WINNER OF THE RITA AWARD
FOR BEST ROMANCE!

Falling Angel by Anne Stuart is a RITA Award winner, voted
Best Romance. A truly wonderful story, *Falling Angel* will
transport you into a world of hidden identities, second
chances and the magic of falling in love.

*"Ms. Stuart's talent shines like the brightest of stars, making
it very obvious that her ultimate destiny is to be the next
romance author at the top of the best-seller charts."*
—*Affaire de Coeur*

A heartwarming story for the holidays. You won't want to miss
award-winning *Falling Angel*, available this January wherever
Harlequin and Silhouette books are sold.

WESTERN *Lovers*

Available in December

**Two more
Western Lovers
ready to rope and tie your heart!**

SAGEBRUSH AND SUNSHINE—
Margot Dalton
Ranchin' Dads
Rodeo champion Gran Lyndon hung up his Stetson
to play daddy to pretty Joanna McLean's son. But
was he going to lose any hope of roping in the
feisty filly the boy called Mom?

RETURN TO YESTERDAY—Annette Broadrick
Reunited Hearts
Felicia St. Clair had returned to Texas to search for
her missing brother, but she wasn't about to fall for
cowboy Dane Rineholt after years of working hard
to forget him. But this time, Dane refused to let
Felicia slip away.

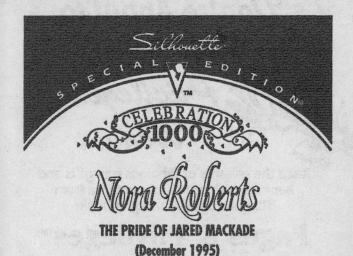

Silhouette

SPECIAL EDITION

™

CELEBRATION 1000

Nora Roberts

THE PRIDE OF JARED MACKADE

(December 1995)

The MacKade Brothers are back! This month,
Jared MacKade's pride is on the line when he
sets his heart on a woman with a past.

If you liked THE RETURN OF RAFE MACKADE (Silhouette
Intimate Moments #631), you'll love Jared's story. Be on
the lookout for the next book in the series, THE HEART OF
DEVIN MACKADE (Silhouette Intimate Moments #697)
in March 1996—with the last MacKade brother's story,
THE FALL OF SHANE MACKADE, coming in April 1996
from Silhouette Special Edition.

These sexy, trouble-loving men
will be heading out to you in
alternating books from Silhouette
Intimate Moments and Silhouette Special Edition.

You're About to Become a *Privileged Woman*

Reap the rewards of fabulous free gifts and benefits with proofs-of-purchase from Silhouette and Harlequin books

Pages & Privileges™

It's our way of thanking you for buying our books at your favorite retail stores.

PROOF OF PURCHASE
Offer expires October 31, 1996
YT-PP81

Pages & Privileges™

Harlequin and Silhouette— the most privileged readers in the world!

For more information about Harlequin and Silhouette's PAGES & PRIVILEGES program call the Pages & Privileges Benefits Desk: 1-503-794-2499

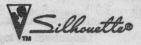

Silhouette®

YT-PP81